"So now I can ask you, dearest Beth, to become my wife."

Beth gasped. Her hand flew to her mouth. "J–John." She could barely utter his name, so shocked was she at his announcement.

"I already know the answer, praise be, just by what was spoken tonight. Forever and amen, you are mine." He again stepped forward, his arms reaching for her, attempting to pull her into his embrace.

"I have hinted at no such thing!" She stepped away, turning from his confused gaze. "You didn't hear what I said at all."

"I heard every word—how you have been waiting for this time as much as I. That I needn't hold myself back any longer. It was like the feel of the ocean breeze to hear you say these words."

"Please. . .I. . ." She paused. "I—I can't marry you."

LAURALEE BLISS, a former nurse, is a prolific writer of inspirational fiction as well as a home educator. She resides with her family near Charlottesville, Virginia, in the foothills of the Blue Ridge Mountains—a place of inspiration for many of her contemporary and historical novels. Lauralee Bliss writes inspirational fiction to provide readers with entertaining stories, intertwined with Christian principles to assist them in their day-to-day walk with the Lord. Aside from writing, she enjoys gardening, cross-stitching, reading, roaming yard sales, and traveling. Lauralee invites you to visit her Web site at www.lauraleebliss.com.

Books by Lauralee Bliss

HEARTSONG PRESENTS
HP249—Mountaintop
HP333—Behind the Mask
HP457—A Rose Among Thorns
HP538—A Storybook Finish
HP569—Ageless Love
HP622—Time Will Tell
HP681—The Wish
HP695—Into the Deep

Don't miss out on any of our super romances. Write to us at the following address for information on our newest releases and club information.

Heartsong Presents Readers' Service
PO Box 721
Uhrichsville, OH 44683

Or visit www.heartsongpresents.com

Journey
to Love

Lauralee Bliss

Heartsong Presents

To Beth McDowell. Thank you for your friendship and your listening ear in my times of need!

A note from the Author:
I love to hear from my readers! You may correspond with me by writing:

Lauralee Bliss
Author Relations
PO Box 721
Uhrichsville, OH 44683

ISBN 978-1-59789-588-0

JOURNEY TO LOVE

All scripture quotations are taken from the King James Version of the Bible.

All of the characters and events in this book are fictitious. Any resemblance to actual persons, living or dead, or to actual events is purely coincidental.

Our mission is to publish and distribute inspirational products offering exceptional value and biblical encouragement to the masses.

PRINTED IN THE U.S.A.

one

Peace I leave with you,
my peace I give unto you:
not as the world giveth, give I unto you.
Let not your heart be troubled, neither let it be afraid.
JOHN 14:27

1650

We now commend the soul of Robert Henry Colman to eternity,
through the name of our Savior Christ. Amen.

It was finished. The chapter drawn to a close. The end of a season and the beginning of the next, like the russet leaves that fall from the trees on the first breath of winter. Beth Colman tried to sleep, but instead, witnessed vision after vision of the burial in her mind. She could still hear the long droning of the minister who had spoken over the coffin of her dead father. She could see the people huddled together, their heads bent, hands folded, the wind ruffling the drab material of their cloaks. Following the departure of all the mourners in attendance at the gravesite, there came to her the smiling face of her older sister, Judith, who seemed unaffected by what had occurred. Even now, Beth couldn't help but frown at the memory. How could Judith smile? Didn't she realize they had just buried the last of their parents? That only the two of them remained out of all their relatives? That all had entered into the heavenly kingdom, leaving them alone in this world?

"There is no need to be alone, Beth," Judith had said to her, pulling the black cloak she wore close about her. "Come stay with Mark and me. I can't bear to think of you at Briarwood any longer."

Beth considered the request, then shook her head. "No. I will be well in time." After all, she had things to do at Briarwood. Father's effects to go through. Times of contemplation, wondering what new chapter would be written in her life, now that this one was finished. As her Savior Christ had spoken—"It is finished."

What will I do next? Her eyes grew accustomed to the ceiling of wood above her, illuminated by the soft, moonlit glow that filled the room. A week had passed since Father's burial, and still she felt barren in purpose. Her life, for so long, had been consumed by Father's needs—fulfilling the duties, no matter how trivial, that his booming voice demanded. Doing what was required to ready him to face a new morning and then assist him to slumber at night. She watched him try to do the simplest things, only to sit, listless, in a chair, unable even to clothe himself in breeches and a shirt. He would say strange things, too. Mutter. Groan. Then speak in an angry voice with an intonation that seemed to shake the very foundation of the solid stone house. During these times, Beth often went into hiding until the episode passed. The physicians who came to see Father had failed to diagnose the strange malady that afflicted him. He toyed with madness, they said. Father seemed trapped in a realm no one could enter. Despite it, Beth could not leave him to his mental instability. She had to help him. He was her father, after all. Even when Judith begged her to let him go, to allow others to care for him so she might live her own life,

Beth had refused. And likewise, after his death, she refused to leave the house but remained to see what else needed to be done.

Beth lay in bed, half-anticipating Father to call out at any moment. Maybe that's why she couldn't sleep nights, even though he was gone. Before his passing, she hadn't slept through a night without his waking her for some request in the midst of a mindless tirade.

"Elizabeth! Fetch me a brandy!"

"Elizabeth! Open the window and let in the night air!"

"Elizabeth! Tell Mother I need her and to come here at once!"

Beth winced and shut her eyes. Oftentimes, Father would call for her mother, who had died long ago. He would ask where she was and why she didn't answer him. At first, Beth couldn't bring herself to tell him Mother was gone from them, taken away when she was still young and beautiful, a victim of the dreaded pox. She feared what it might do to Father's already tortured mind. And so, much as she hated to speak a mistruth, she rationalized her words as being for her father's greater good and claimed Mother had gone to market, was out visiting friends, or having a new gown made. Father soon realized, however, something was amiss. He had a worried and wild look about him. When she finally did tell him that Mother had left to be with God, Father broke down and cried.

A tear drifted down her cheek. Beth quickly wiped it away. Judith was right. She shouldn't stay here in this huge house, which seemed more like a tomb than a home, with her thoughts consumed by memories. She must seek a new path for herself, but what?

After a fitful night, the rays of morning sunshine proved a

welcome sight. While the sun should have cheered her, she felt nothing. If only she didn't feel so unsure, so useless with idle hands and a vacant heart. Looking into Father's room that morning, she expected to find him in bed, his gray eyes focused on the ceiling, a frown painted on his grizzled face, awaiting her assistance. "Help me up, Elizabeth!" his gravely voice would demand. With the help of the servants, she would escort him to a chair that would become his place of rest for a good part of the day, by a window overlooking Briarwood's famous gardens. She would read him a passage of scripture. Fetch him the day's meals. And pray that whatever ailed him would be gone forever.

And now, her father's mind, body, and soul were brought to peace by the merciful hand of death.

Beth wandered about the halls until she found her personal servant, Josephine, setting out the morning victuals. The lump in her throat quenched any hope of an appetite. She only took a bit of crust from the bread and forced it down her throat.

"I'm so sorry for all this, Miss," Josephine said with a sigh. "How can I help?"

"We will clear my father's room today," Beth announced. "And then I will see if Lord Addington is still of a notion to acquire Briarwood. 'Tis only right and good for us to do what needs to be done. He once loved this place. He will take proper care of it, I'm certain."

Josephine nearly upset the pitcher she was carrying. "Oh, must we leave?"

"You know we can't remain here any longer."

"I suppose I shall seek out my family in London, then. But begging your pardon, Miss, where will you go?"

The words echoed in her mind. *Where will you go,*

Elizabeth Anne Colman? What will become of you? "I suppose I shall marry," she said with a half-hearted laugh. "If it's not too late." The chuckle faded away. Again came the memories of suitors who paid visits—the sons of Father's aristocratic friends, even a second cousin, all interested and looking to discover if Elizabeth Colman might be ready to exchange this life for one of marital bliss. And in each instance, she had refused their intentions. Father would ask why all the young men were paying calls to Briarwood. She would tell him they had hoped to find an eligible woman for marriage. Father would take her hand in his, his gray eyes pleading, and beg in a scratchy voice for her not to leave him.

She'd abided by his wishes. . .until now, after his death, when the door had suddenly been thrust open before her. What else was there to do but marry?

"I fear it may be too late for some of the callers, Miss," Josephine said with sorrow evident in her voice. "Many have left England, or so I've heard. My lord master Austin. My lord master Billings. To that new land, they are going. The land far away across the ocean, the one called Virginia."

Beth frowned. "As if some new land could bring happiness," she murmured. "Then I suppose I'm too late for everything. . . even for love."

"Nay. I don't believe that. 'Tis never too late for love, especially from our God who knows when the time is right. 'Stir not up, nor awake my love, until he please.' And I know that time is soon upon you, Miss."

Josephine's words proved soothing on a day already filled with uncertainty. How Beth would miss her when she took her leave of this place. They had become more like sisters through the care of her father, even if Josephine was only a servant by status. Yet Beth knew the girl was so much more. While her sister, Judith, had left to marry and set up her own house, Beth found in Josephine a true heart and listening ear as in no other.

Just then, Beth heard a friendly greeting in the foyer. The pleasantry echoed throughout the manor home. She hurried to find Judith there, alongside her husband, Mark. Beth envied her sister for finding such a man as Mark Reynolds. Tall and stout, with golden locks, fashionably dressed in baggy breeches, a ruffled white shirt, and short waistcoat accented with lace, he was the perfect portrait of a gentleman. Her sister stood with her arm linked through his, appearing content and peaceful, her dream of love and happiness fulfilled—all of it making Beth's heart ache.

Judith immediately took Beth's pale hands in hers. Her sister's were warm and inviting, while Beth's hands were as frigid as the winter snow. They walked together down the cold and dank hall to the sitting room. "I'm so sorry for all you have been through, dear sister," Judith said. "I couldn't sleep for thinking of you."

At least the merciful words brought the assurance that someone cared. "I'm well. You needn't worry about me."

"Oh, but I do worry. I know this must be hard. You were devoted to Father for a very long time. Though we shall miss him, we must think of tomorrow." She paused. "*Your* tomorrow, dear Beth."

Beth looked away, to a tapestry hanging on the wall. It had been one of their mother's favorites, of the English countryside filled with the flowers of springtime. It spoke of beauty and life. Beth hoped to take it with her wherever she went. Suddenly she caught herself. *Take it with me where, pray tell? Where shall I go? What will I do? What will be my tomorrow when I can't see past yesterday?*

At that moment Mark joined them, quietly occupying one of the sturdy chairs nearby. "We have been thinking," Judith continued, acknowledging her husband. "We hadn't spoken of this since Father took ill, but we believe the time has come."

Beth watched the two of them share silent communication through their gazes as it seemed only married people could do.

"My husband and I have decided to leave England."

"Leave England!" Beth repeated. "I don't understand. Where are you going?"

"You know our country is in turmoil right now. Many of our friends have found themselves persecuted for their status and their ties to the former crown. One of my lord's closest friends has even been falsely imprisoned." She drew in a breath. "We can't live under this, nor do we wish it upon our children yet to be begotten. So we have decided to take our leave of this place, to board a ship at Portsmouth and remove ourselves to Virginia."

Beth stared, unable to believe what she was hearing. Leave their homeland? The place of their birth? The land where they had been raised and the land that now cradled the earthly remains of both their parents, though their souls embraced eternity? "But how can you leave?"

Judith stirred in her seat. "We believe it's for the best. And we want to fulfill a dream of Father's."

"What dream is this? He never spoke of going to Virginia."

"You may not know this, Beth, but he wrote often of his curiosity with regard to his own parents. Our grandparents. Where they had gone. What might have become of them."

"Your grandparents were part of the lost colony," Mark added. "The one that settled in the place called Roanoke, in the land of Hatorask. We have the opportunity of finding out what might have happened to them."

"But that was so long ago," Beth said. "No one knows what happened."

"We can try, Beth," Judith implored. "Though Father is gone from us, I know he would approve if we sought to find out what happened. Perhaps even now we have family relations who live in the new land of Virginia. Aunts and uncles we have never embraced. Cousins, even. We must find out if we're truly alone or if there are others we may not know about."

Beth could not help but fly to her feet. "But why? We have just buried Father. How can you leave me and this place?"

Judith stood to her feet as well, her hand outstretched. "We don't plan to leave you. We want you to come with us to Virginia. Beth, consider. There is nothing for you here. Even now our country stirs with rising conflict. Men fighting each other for selfish gain. I don't want us to be here, caught up in the suffering. Virginia is safe. And there we can find the answers to our family, to the mystery that plagued Father for so long, while we make a new home for ourselves."

Beth fell silent. Her mind struggled to understand all of the considerations suddenly thrust upon her. Never had she heard Father speak about a longing to discover what happened to his parents. Perhaps he had, but she had been so consumed by other things—maybe she hadn't listened. And maybe that longing in his heart had furthered the illness in his mind.

Glancing up to see the pleading in her sister's eyes, Beth couldn't help but be stirred by what she said. She wanted so much to know what would happen with her life now that Father was gone. And the adventure would be a welcome change. Could the answer lie with a voyage to some distant land? "But is it truly safe, this Virginia?" Beth wondered.

"Sister, doesn't God lead us to safety, to His strong tower? I believe He is leading us, as He has led others to find life in a new world."

He has led others to find life in a new world. Her gaze traveled to the tapestry. Perhaps buds of hope and purpose were about to blossom, if she could only find the courage to embrace them.

❧

With her knees weak and her stomach still heaving from the tossing of the ship, Beth was thankful to feel firm ground beneath her feet. They had finally completed the treacherous voyage across the ocean to the bustling port called Jamestown in Virginia. All around were the sounds of men toting barrels and exchanging loud chatter. Many stared at her as if she were fresh produce in the market. Animals wandered about in the street. The sharp scents of a foreign place filled her nostrils. Her senses were overwhelmed, sending her thoughts tumbling away. Between the voyage and, now, the activity of this strange land, Beth was desperate to find a quiet place to recover from all she had endured. *Would such a wish prove too difficult to fulfill?*

At least she was thankful to see her brother-in-law take up the reins of leadership, seeing to their comfort by inquiring of a place for them to stay until they could find a place of their own. When Mark learned from passersby of a family that allowed weary travelers to stay among them, he escorted Beth and Judith at once to the Worthington Tavern. It looked rustic to Beth—a mere commoner's dwelling made of clapboards, the thatched roof constructed from reeds that grew thick on the shore. She pulled her wrap tighter as if trying to shield herself from this place. How different it all appeared from the thick stone walls of the manor home of Briarwood framed by the lush English countryside. At least the inn had a solid wood floor and not a swaying ship deck, which had left her feeling dizzy still.

Beth entered the tavern to see a long table and several men slurping down food from wooden bowls. She tried to keep her attention elsewhere but couldn't help noticing a man who sat at the end of the table. His gaze had been clearly focused on her when she entered. Again, she drew her wrap tighter around her. It had been a long time since a man looked at her in such a way. Not since the suitors who paid calls during her father's illness. A very long time ago indeed. But this was neither the time nor the place to think of suitors. This was not her beloved England, either, but a new place inhabited by strange people—and strange men.

Suddenly the man left the table and approached Mark. "Good day, my lord. My name is John Harris. You just arrived on the ship from England?"

"Yes. I'm Mark Reynolds. This is my wife, Judith, and my sister-in-law, Beth."

The man named John nodded to her, but Beth looked away, pretending to stare at the simple, rough-hewn walls that comprised the humble house. When she looked back, he was still staring at her, as if appreciating some marvelous painting. The thought made her blush. She chastised herself for such a vain thought.

"Perhaps you can help us, Master Harris," Mark continued. "We are most interested in seeking out a place called Hatorask. The area where the colony of Roanoke was said to exist. Have you heard of it or know of anyone who has?"

"Hatorask!" Beth could see the fire ignite in the man's

blue eyes and his lips upturn into a smile that displayed good teeth. "I know the place well. Why are you interested in the Hatorask region, my lord?"

" 'Tis a family matter."

"I see. I can assist you in your journey, if you wish."

Mark smiled. "Blessed be the Lord! Surely He has guided our footsteps. Very good. We will talk further." Mark turned and whispered to Judith.

"Come, Beth, let us find a place to rest," Judith urged, taking her arm.

"What business does your husband have with a stranger?" Beth wondered aloud.

"My lord is beside himself," she said with a chuckle. "He wishes to find out about our relatives as soon as possible, before we settle here. He seeks a guide to lead us to where the colony once existed."

"But. . .we have only just arrived! And I'm so weary. . . ." Her voice faded away. *Please, dear Lord, just a moment's rest. A small fragment of peace.*

"There will be plenty of time to rest. There are plans to make. It would do us well to accomplish the journey while we can, before we see to a home." She sighed. "And I can't stop the passion within him. When Mark first heard of this mystery within our family, it moved him unlike anything I have ever seen. He will not be stilled until we have found the answers. And I must admit I want to find the answers, too. I want to know if we have relatives here."

"These ideas of a journey and exploration, discovery and mystery seem to move every man," Beth commented, thinking of the way John Harris responded at the mere mention of the Hatorask region. "I even saw it in the stranger's eyes."

"It does. 'Tis what made this place, after all. Men and

women with a dream who came to this land despite the great odds. Like our grandparents. And so it is God's will that we come here to make new lives. I believe it." Judith gently squeezed her hand. "He will bless us, sweet sister."

"I hope you are right," Beth said softly. "But can we just sit for a moment and breathe without having to endure another journey?"

Judith laughed. "Only for a moment, until my husband returns. Then we will soon be off on our next grand adventure."

Beth sighed. Just as she feared. If only she could find a place of refuge. Perhaps she should have remained in Cambridge, even if it was inside the cold stone walls of Briarwood with all its memories. At least it was calm and quiet there. Here, she was at the mercy of her zealous brother-in-law and strangers, such as the man named John, who stared at her with blue eyes, which bored into her very soul. "Merciful God, please help me."

two

John Harris thought long and hard of the encounter at the tavern last evening. How like a doe did the sister-in-law of the gentleman Reynolds appear. Graceful and purposeful but shy. Unsure of her surroundings. Fearful of strangers. Vulnerable. Try as he might, he could not dismiss her from his thoughts. He wanted to reach out and reassure her, to make her feel welcome and at ease with these strange surroundings. If only he could.

Though he had been here for many years now, he still recalled his own uncertainty the first time he stepped onto this new land. He was just as much a frightened animal of the forest as she seemed to be. But it didn't take long for him to fall into the company of men looking to explore the lands that stretched out beyond Jamestown and the great James River. They were eager to find what existed to the very horizon. The tiny flame of desire to explore soon became a raging fire. Wherever his feet were destined to tread, he would go. And he went. Fast and far to the region known as Hatorask. And on his heels came his brother, Robert, likewise an adventurer, following in his shadow, learning all he could at the tender age of sixteen, even if he were a bit impetuous at times.

There was a great interest to explore back then and little time to contemplate having a home and family. Until now, when John returned to Jamestown to see families sprouting like vegetables in a garden. Hearing the laughter of little ones playing with their balls and hoops in the town square. Watching the farms begin to dot the countryside; the fields fairly bursting with tobacco and corn. Witnessing it all, John decided the time had come for him to likewise plant roots. He would give up exploration and seek a life with the woman God had chosen for him.

John ventured often to the port of Jamestown where the ships docked. Many bore eligible women called "tobacco brides," arranged for those who sought wives through the payment of tobacco harvested from the fields. He had neither tobacco fields nor a home, nary a shilling to his name. But it didn't deter him. Watching the women arrive in the shallops from the great ships anchored in the bay, he prayed for the right one to call his own. *Lord, show me the one You have chosen to be my bride.*

Then the shallop arrived, bearing the graceful doe of Miss Colman. He could still see her so clearly when she stood at the docks. Her hands had been trembling, her eyes wide as she looked about the new land. He wanted to go forward at that moment and offer a greeting to calm her fear. Instead, he retreated into the background and walked to the tavern for his meal, all the while hoping he would see the young woman again soon. And suddenly, she was there, right at the doorstep. His heart couldn't help but leap at such an answer to prayer. She didn't seem to notice him, but that would change once they made their acquaintance. He would make certain of it.

John consumed his drink in the pewter tumbler before focusing his attention on the man sitting opposite him who had introduced himself as Mark Reynolds. Like himself, there was a passion within the man to see beyond the outer regions. And now the man sought a guide to take him to the

Hatorask region in the land called the province of Carolana, the windswept land of sand by the ocean, many miles south of Jamestown. John could not believe his fortune at meeting someone interested in the very place he once explored.

"So you are willing to guide us to Hatorask for this price, Master Harris?" Mark inquired, showing him a purse of money.

John nodded. The money was fine, yes, but the journey was even better. At least for now he did not have to think about settling here by the James River. There would be plenty of time for such things. Now it seemed God had sent Mark Reynolds to renew his own fervor for exploration. "And what of the women in your company, my lord? Will they also make the journey?" He could not steady the rapid beating of his heart. *The truth be known, will your sister-in-law be coming along?* He hoped she would be there to brighten the journey with her presence. Perhaps he could have both—not only a trip to Hatorask, but also a woman to one day call his own.

"Of course. We seek their relatives. Is there a manner of difficulty with this?"

"Oh no, not at all." He hoped he didn't sound too eager. He didn't wish to reveal his interest in the fair young woman that was the gentleman's sister-in-law. Like the new land, he wanted very much to discover her true beauty and worth, which now lay hidden beneath a cloak of fear and uncertainty—and to give her a small measure of the confidence she needed to survive in this place.

For himself, he might have been too confident after the time spent here. Too sure of his abilities. And the pride cost him dearly, forging a wound that nothing could heal. John looked away. He didn't want to reveal that aching in his soul. Why it came forth now, he didn't know. He pushed it aside, especially when he saw the gentleman gazing at him as if wanting to discover his personal land of heartache and grief. John would not allow him to find it. Nor any woman either. The matter lay deep within himself, and there it would remain.

"Well, I thank our Sovereign God that we found you, Master Harris."

"Please call me John." He offered his hand.

"And you may call me Mark. As I said, 'tis indeed providential we have met. To find a man that knows this land of Hatorask where the colony of Roanoke once existed and can guide us to the very place. . .quite remarkable."

"You realize that no trace of the colony has been found except for a few belongings left behind in haste and some strange word carved in a tree. They are very much gone forever."

Mark only smiled as if the news proved inconsequential. "I believe there is an answer somewhere, just waiting to be discovered. And with you leading us, John Harris, I'm all the more confident we will find what we're seeking."

John marveled. A cheerful and confident man indeed. No doubt commanded by his Savior. If only John felt such things in his own life.

"And have you found success here in this land, Master Harris?"

"If you mean do I own lands and a home, no. There is more to success than the possessions one gains."

"I agree. We have but a few possessions ourselves as we didn't want to be burdened by them on such a long voyage. We are beginning anew." He sighed. "It is just as well. England has become a den of thieves. There are those willing to squeeze the life out of their brothers because of jealousy.

It is good to come here with little, to begin again as if a paintbrush to a clean canvas."

John immediately liked the man sitting before him. Mark offered words of wisdom. He wasn't pretentious. And he was eager to hire John for a trip that fed his desire to explore once again.

"Thank you." Mark stood to his feet and extended his hand, which John shook. "A pleasure doing business."

"Likewise." John offered a farewell and ventured out of the tavern into the bright sunshine. A fine spring day it was turning out to be, although the summers here could be unbearable. He wondered how the fair Miss Colman would take to a new place that proved much different from her native England. He knew that a strange land tested faith with periods of doubt and hoped he might help renew that faith and cast any doubt into the sea.

With the sun shining full in his face, he thought of the time he first stepped off a shallop onto this land, wondering if he had made the right choice. If he would succeed in this place. If he would make the money he needed to pay off his debts. But the exuberance of his younger brother overshadowed any of his doubts. Like Mark Reynolds this day, his brother, Robert, was a cheerful soul, teeming with confidence no matter what lay before him.

"What a fine place this is!" Robert had said, the grin spreading from cheek to cheek, his zeal infectious. " 'Tis not a fine place indeed, John? Will we see all of it?"

"All of it and more, Robert." *Better to agree,* he thought. When he did say the words, he felt his confidence rise. He believed they would see all of the land. They would lead a victorious life, and they would claim it for God and for country.

But little did we know, this fine place is also an unpredictable place—a place that could birth dreams only to have them taken away. A place of danger and death.

John walked the muddy road between the homes made of clapboard or simple sticks held together with mud. He tried not to dwell on the past until he saw a vivid reminder of it all, standing there before him. He stopped short. They were not often seen in Jamestown after many of the uprisings that had occurred. Now there were two of them. One even wore an English hat of all things. The shiny black hair reflected the rays of sunlight. The skins of animals that clad their glistening frames looked fresh, as did the painted faces. John tried to shift his thoughts to peaceful things, to dwell on the things above and not on the Indians before him, but he couldn't. The mere sight of them stirred up raw feelings within, feelings he had not been able to relinquish eighteen months later. His wound was still fresh, as if it had happened yesterday. He wanted to look aside and continue on but kept staring at the Indians instead. They had goods in their possession. Obviously they had just finished bartering—obtaining pots, beads, and other trinkets for baskets of corn. And that is not all they traded. They traded lives as well—colonist for Indian, Indian for colonist. Lives torn apart. Blood spilled fresh. The faces and voices known so well, gone forever.

John hurried away before the anger he had fought to control rose with a vengeance, leaving peace in the dust. Only then did he hear his name hailed. He turned to see a fellow explorer of the southern regions, Samuel Wright, calling to him from across the street.

"John Harris. And where are you off to in such a hurry?"

He was glad for the interruption and silently thanked

God. "Good to see you, my friend. I have great news to tell. I'm going back to Hatorask."

"Are you now? And why, pray tell? I thought you were going to settle here with the bride of your choosing."

"I've been hired to lead a family there. A man that just arrived on the ship yesterday. And two women."

"Two women, eh? Why are you burdening yourself with such travelers?" He paused before a grin spread wide across his face. "Unless. . .could it be? Have you now turned your heart to settling down with a bride at Hatorask? A dream about to be fulfilled?"

John admitted he once thought of settling in the land by the ocean, without another living soul inhabiting the place for miles. But it was hardly the place to put up a home or to bring a wife, lest he could convince his lady that Hatorask would be a fine place to settle. And yet look what he was about to do—lead a family that had an eligible woman among them to Hatorask.

"Ah, I can see it. That is exactly what you wish to do, isn't it? To see if perhaps you may have found what you've been seeking?"

"I'm only hired to guide them there," John insisted. "And I haven't spoken to her."

Samuel shook his head. "Then tell me, why guide them to that place in particular? There are no settlements. Nothing but Indians and a few fools like us, searching in vain for treasure."

"They are seeking relatives lost with the colony at Roanoke."

"What?" Samuel waved his hand. " 'Tis a long journey for a foolish dream. The people there died long ago. Killed by the Indians, they were." He blanched. "Forgive me, John. The words came out in haste. I didn't think. . . ."

"It matters not. But the gentleman, Reynolds, the one who hired me, seems to think there may still be answers left to find. He is like us, Samuel. He wants to explore. Adventure is a part of him. And even if his quest leads nowhere, the fact that it leads to Hatorask is good enough for me."

"And I'm sure a bit of money to fill your pocket makes a good convincer, as well."

John grinned. "Money speaks quite loudly. I have debts left in England that the purse will surely cover."

"Then I wish you Godspeed on this new journey of yours. And. . .be careful."

Samuel's words held an ominous ring to them. John once thought himself the most prudent individual regarding everything he put his mind to—until he threw caution to the wind and tragedy reared its head. John tried not to blame himself, but he did. He was supposed to be the protector, after all. The leader. The one who held lives in his hands. And he let it slip away. His inattentiveness had cost him dearly, more than any money could buy or any exploration to Hatorask could do. Only God Himself could bear the true pain of it all.

Don't do this to yourself, John. Don't or it will destroy you. You know this to be true. Let this rest in the Almighty's care. Cast thy burdens upon the Lord, for He cares for you.

He tried to focus his thoughts on the surroundings—the people bustling about, those sharing pleasantries with each another, the sound of bleating sheep, the conversation of men working the nearby dock—anything to rid his mind of the past and the scenes that plagued both his waking and his sleep.

Then he caught sight of her once more, and everything else left him. He rubbed his eyes to make certain he wasn't dreaming. She was indeed Miss Colman, walking along the opposite side of the street with her sister. He watched the women carry themselves with grace and dignity, careful to avoid the people and the roaming animals. Miss Colman held tight to her wrap as if it were some great shield protecting her. Her sister talked endlessly about something—what, John couldn't determine. He drew closer. Miss Colman looked pretty in what bit of the gown he saw below the wrap— although too fancy for these surroundings. Brown curls rested on her shoulders. She was perfect, if cautious. He inhaled a breath. He must make her feel at ease. After all, they would soon be journeying to Hatorask together. It would be good to make their acquaintance as soon as possible.

He began walking toward them, only to stop short when he heard them conversing in a disagreeing tone.

"If only I knew someone here," Miss Colman mourned. "I don't like this. I would stay here if I could and let you both go on this grand adventure of yours. I have no interest in it."

"There is nothing to fear. My lord has already told me he has found an excellent guide. Don't you wish to discover what happened to our family? Our grandparents?"

John watched her draw the wrap even tighter about her, outlining the curve of her upper arms. Her hands were lily white in color, her face even more so against her large brown eyes as she stared at her sister. Her eyes gleamed with intensity, almost as if tears might be clouding them. John shook his head. This would never do. He couldn't bear to see her cry.

He came up. "Hello, my ladies. Welcome to Jamestown."

Miss Colman cried in a start and whirled about, her hand covering her mouth. "Sir, you should have made your presence known!"

"Dearest Beth, he did," the sister admonished her, then turned to John. "Thank you, sir."

"I just spoke with your husband about the journey to Hatorask, madam," he said to the sister. "John Harris, at your bidding."

"So you are our guide! My husband speaks highly of your knowledge, Mr. Harris."

When he looked at Beth, as her sister called her, her gaze loomed elsewhere. She couldn't look at him straightway—almost as if he had an evil appearance or a face marred by the pox. If only she would look at him, and yes, appreciate what she saw. He very much appreciated her comeliness. "I'm eager to show you the land. 'Tis handsome indeed."

"I hope you can help us with our quest, as well," said the sister.

John readied himself to speak of their quest at finding out about the Roanoke Colony—a rather foolish notion in his opinion. Instead he only smiled and nodded. He was not about to cause a further rift between them all. He now turned to Beth. How he liked her name. "I trust you fared well on your journey here from England, madam?"

"I was ill every day," Beth complained. "The sailors were a vile lot. They cursed and were drunk. I feared for my virtue." She cast him a quick glance as if she were comparing him to such men. He winced at the thought. He wanted only to soothe her fears, to tell her she could trust him. But even if he were to say the right words, she might not believe him. She had to be convinced by deed and not by word alone.

"But God protected us," the sister admonished. "He is our shield and strong tower. And now we are very much anticipating our journey to the southern regions, Mr. Harris." She paused. "Perhaps you would do us the favor of joining us for dinner at the tavern so we may further discuss the trip? I think it would set all our minds at ease to hear of your exploits."

He bowed. "It would be my pleasure, madam." He hoped for a nod of approval from Beth but received none. *Give me but a few moments, Miss Beth Colman, and I will ease all your misgivings.*

"We look forward to seeing you again." With a nod the sister proceeded on, Beth following close behind, but not before Beth cast him one final glance. It was that glance that stayed with John, sparking hope in his restless heart.

three

"Why did you invite that stranger to eat with us?" Beth moaned to Judith. She held up the looking glass to examine her hair, which she painstakingly arranged in a chignon with ringlets framing her cheeks.

"If we are going on this journey, you do believe it's wise to find out more about our guide, don't you?"

"Don't you trust your husband that our guide is a man of excellence?"

"Of course I do. I only invited him in the hope he might ease your fears. It's not like you hide them well, Elizabeth Anne."

Beth frowned at the utterance of her full name. She had heard from her parents how they named her after the former queen of England, partly for the reddish highlights in her brown hair, but mostly for her fiery spirit to live. Her delivery had been difficult, from what she had been told. The midwife said when she was born, she was small, spindly, and would not live to see tomorrow. And yet here she was a grown woman, healthy in mind and body, if a bit troubled in spirit. She only wished Judith wouldn't make light of her concerns. She had been through a great deal these many years. Was it not proper and right for her to consider these plans in light of everything?

"I do not fear," Beth denied. "I only want to be certain this journey you and your husband are planning is indeed the will of the Almighty and not some vain quest that will only bring disappointment. Consider this. Wouldn't you rather settle down, Judith? Make a fine home in a dwelling that your husband will build for you? Have a large garden? Raise young ones? I very much would like a niece or a nephew."

"Of course I want all that. Every woman does."

Beth leaned closer. "Then why this trip? Why must we go to Hatorask now? You and I can stay here and let the men go on the quest. There is no reason for us to go, too."

"I will not leave my husband. And I will not leave you here alone in this place. So unseemly. How can you even think such things? Can you not bear to consider this one final duty? 'Tis our relatives we seek, after all. Do you not want to know if we have family here? That we are not alone in this world after losing both Father and Mother?"

"I know nothing of our grandparents. Father was but a lad when they left to come here. It was so long ago. What does it matter if we find out what happened to them?"

"It matters to our family. And it once mattered to our father."

"He never spoke of it to me. If this issue lay so heavy on his heart, I'm certain he would have said something. Maybe you dreamed it so you might go on some grand adventure."

Judith said no more but strode over to the trunk sitting in the corner of the room. She opened it slowly, sifting through the few items they brought from England. When she reached their mother's folded tapestry, Beth helped her take it out. She inhaled a sharp breath when she saw it—the symbol of all she had lost and all she had left behind.

"What do you seek?" she asked Judith. "The tapestry?"

"You will see." From the bottom of the chest, Judith withdrew a tattered book, the leather worn, the pages falling out of the thread binding that barely held it together.

"What is that?" Beth wondered.

"You've never seen this, I'm certain. As the eldest, I was given Father's journal from Mother, who asked me to keep it safe. Father wrote in it faithfully when he was young. He speaks of many things on his heart, but especially about a few things I believe you will find interesting." She opened it carefully. A cloud of dust from ages past rose up, bringing with it the aroma of history and the lure of unanswered questions.

Judith began reading. " 'This night I think of my parents taken from me. Yes, I do care for my great-aunt and uncle who have raised me, but I think this night of my parents and their journey to the New World to be a part of the new colony. Uncle William spoke of their yearning to see a new place. But they never returned. I wish I knew what happened to them.' " Judith paused. "There now. Do you see how much this meant to Father?"

Beth looked over Judith's shoulder to examine the pages, the ink smeared and barely legible. She traced the print of her father's hand and his thoughts inscribed on the paper for memory's sake. "But this writing was done long ago, and the intent forgotten, just like this colony that our grandparents helped to found. From what I've heard, nothing was ever found of the colonists but for a few clues after Governor White returned. Some tried to find the survivors, but to no avail. Why should we hope for any greater success?"

" 'Tis the least we can do to satisfy Father's wish. Can we do no less while we have the means? Who knows what may happen? Mark is eager to go forth. And if this man, Master Harris, was brought by God to be our guide, surely the Lord's hand is already on this journey."

Judith closed the book and set it on the chest, urging

Beth to hurry and come downstairs before the guide arrived for the meal. Once she left, Beth slowly opened the book, smelling the earthy odor of age. She noted Father's distinct handwriting.

Uncle William says I must bury these thoughts I have for my parents, that they are in a better place, with God in heaven. I wish I could, but something in me yearns to know. When I am older, I will buy my own passage to the New World and find out what happened. They are my flesh and blood, after all. My parents. Even if Uncle William has no understanding of what lies inside me, I must know what happened. 'Tis the only way to find peace.

A strange feeling came over Beth after reading these written words. *'Tis the only way to find peace.* Dare she even consider that Father's tortured mind might have been further burdened by this pain from long ago? Now that he was gone, had God opened the door to make it possible for his children—she and Judith—to seek the answer for him? If only she could know.

Beth sighed and closed the book. Enough contemplation. Their guest would arrive any time now. She peered once more at the small looking glass that displayed her features. Her brown eyes were wide and thoughtful, the sunlight through the small window igniting the strands of red in her hair. Yet fear toyed with her over the thought of traveling to another unknown place. If only she could convince Judith to allow her to stay behind while she went to fulfill their father's dream. Perhaps Beth could still stay here if she found a room with an older woman. Maybe this John would know of someone who would take her in. Or perhaps she could stay and help the family that served as the proprietors of this place. Though the tavern where they remained certainly was plain and not in keeping with the grandeur she was accustomed to, it would suffice as a place of refuge.

Beth set down the looking glass. It was not to be. Judith would never agree. And in her heart, she knew Father would want her to be a part of this family quest. There was no choice in the matter. This journey to Hatorask was also her journey—a journey of the heart and spirit.

❧

They had already taken their seats at the dining table in a small room when Beth arrived. She gave a quick greeting and stiff curtsy, with her back straight and hands folded, before taking her place at the table. She sincerely hoped John Harris would not stare at her as he had during their last meeting. Many men in this place of Jamestown looked at her with interest, as if marriage were foremost in their minds. Judith laughed it away, saying they were but lonely men. Few women graced the new land. It was to be expected, after all. But the attention made Beth uneasy, wishing she knew more about relationships; how she should act, what she should say. No doubt their dinner guest would be more than willing to give a few lessons in such etiquette. She had seen his gaze, both when she arrived and when they met on the street. He appeared overly eager to make her acquaintance.

But at that moment, John was not staring at her but rather the food placed on the table—rarebit with cornbread on the side. When the blessing was said, he eagerly helped himself to a large portion and began eating as if he had never tasted food. She watched in dismay as he held his spoon like a club and shoveled down the food with all the appearance of a ravenous animal. When he looked up and noticed her obvious disdain, he set down his spoon.

"Forgive me, madam. Rarely have I had the chance to eat in the presence of such beautiful ladies."

Judith laughed. " 'Tis good to see a man enjoying the victuals."

Beth was about to make a comment to the contrary, but instead, she picked up her spoon and took a dainty bite. After a few minutes, she glanced up to find a smirk painted on John's face.

"I fear you will be dining most of the evening if you indulge in such modest amounts with each bite, madam."

"But at least I will have the pleasure of tasting my food, sir."

He sat back, the smirk widening into a grin. "You have wit. And here I thought you fearful as a rabbit."

"So long as I'm not someone's intended prey." Beth bent once more over her food but could clearly see that this John no longer seemed interested in eating. His gaze was now set upon her.

"I agree. How do you wish to be seen, madam?"

"As someone of worth, just as the eyes of the Lord see me."

His face relaxed, his blue eyes muted as if a fog had drifted over them. "A wise answer. As you wish."

Beth felt her face grow warm. He had fallen for her very words. Now what was she to do?

The moment was broken by a loud cough. Mark gestured to John with his goblet.

"So tell us about this place called Hatorask, Master Harris. I wish to know everything there is to know."

"Where do I begin, my lord? 'Tis better to see it for yourself than for me to try to describe it. But if you can imagine a land with no homes or people but only the call of the gulls and the roar of the ocean, you would be correct."

Beth put down her spoon to think on the scene he had painted with his words. Cambridge had been far away from the sea. Except for the voyage here, when the pounding of waves against the ship was the common sound, she had not been acquainted with the ocean. "Why are there no settlements?" she asked.

"There was once a charter for settlement set forth by the late King Charles I. But politics within England have changed, as you know. The king is dead and so, too, is the charter he once gave to settle the province called Carolana. For now, men are content to explore the region until there is a permanent charter." He paused. "But there will be settlements soon, I'm certain. Jamestown is filling with people. Some have established homes northward along the James River. But there are also increasing tensions with the Indians of this land. Settling the southern regions seems to be the open door at the moment."

"Have there been many conflicts with the naturals?" Mark wondered.

"There are times of tension and times of peace, if one could call a cessation of hostilities peace. The last hostility was a few years ago. Still, I do not wish to associate with them. They hold to devilish practices."

"Surely they are but poor, lost souls," Beth commented.

"They may be lost, madam, but they are in command of their weapons and with a will to use them. There have been treaties signed at different times, but none have lasted for very long. Men seek peace only to suffer in the aftermath. 'Tis best to remain on guard, for you never know what will happen while you're looking the other way."

Beth tried to focus her gaze on her meal but found her

thoughts adrift like a ship at sea. If he was trying to allay her fears, this description didn't help in the least. Now she had new fears to consider.

"I'm certain one must be on their guard in England, too," John added. "There are plenty of rogues and scoundrels in this world."

"Indeed," Mark commented. "With the change of hands in the English government, we found our very existence threatened in our own country. The common man is seen as the one in need of justice, and those with wealth are seen as a scourge."

"Is that why you left?"

"And our father died," Judith added. "The time for change had come. Not only the political changes in our homeland but also the changes in our families moved us to seek a new life. And since Beth once cared for our father day and night, it seemed good for us to leave and begin again."

Once more Beth felt the gaze of John linger on her. "I'm certain your circumstance must have been difficult for you," he said softly in her direction.

"No more difficult than what we are about to undertake with this expedition," she murmured. All at once she felt a slight touch and jumped at the sensation. John's fingers had come to rest lightly on top of her hand.

"Madam, you have no need to fear while I'm here. Yes, the journey to Hatorask is long. But once you're there, the place will captivate you." He removed his hand and exhaled. "It did me. I was not without uncertainty, but soon the land did enchant me with its wonders. And to know that God wishes for us to be happy, to build our lives, to make this place mighty for His Name's sake. 'Tis all good."

Beth couldn't help but lift her gaze to meet his. She saw

the crook of a smile form on his lips. He was indeed a good Christian gentleman, speaking words of assistance and hope that stirred up her curiosity. "So you will see to our safety?"

"With my life." He then took up a piece of cornbread Judith passed to him.

Beth could barely eat after this. While Mark and John continued to talk about the land of Virginia and the province of Carolana where Hatorask lay, Beth marveled at John's interesting characteristics. Perhaps a journey in his company might do her good. She could find out more about him and inquire of God whether a blessed union waited on the wings of her future.

When John bid them farewell that evening, Judith immediately ventured over to Beth and smiled. "Well, it seems as though you and Mr. Harris have each made one another's acquaintance. Perhaps too well, if appearances are not deceiving."

Beth flushed at the implication. "He was only trying to reassure me."

"I could see that quite plainly. Every word you spoke, he held it close to his heart. And I must say you also seemed interested in his words."

"Maybe only in that I still hold some manner of attractiveness to men." She was surprised at the tears that welled up. Day after day, night after night, caring for her father while watching suitors come and go with hunched shoulders and sad expressions, she couldn't help but wonder if the status of the unmarried, such as Queen Elizabeth, would also be her lot. Maybe she would be forever married to principle and to place, wherever that place might be. That was, until now, with the attention of John Harris renewing hope.

"I know you have been through much in your young life,

Beth. But now is the time to reach out with your faith and embrace what God has planned for you. There are great things waiting for you. Surely you can feel it."

"I only hope I'm ready."

Judith embraced her. "God knows the times and the seasons. Open your heart, Beth, and you will find the season of love when you least expect it."

A season of love, like the blooming English garden woven into Mother's tapestry. She sighed. How lovely that would be. If only she did not find herself doubting the words.

four

"Every word you spoke, he held it close to his heart. And. . .you also seemed interested. . . ."

Beth reflected over the words spoken by her sister. Could it be so plain to Judith and everyone else that some manner of attraction was there? She hardly knew John Harris. They had just met and only because Mark hired him. Was he like all the men she had seen walking about the streets of Jamestown, a man desperate to find a wife and establish himself? Or were these the natural bonds of love that only God Himself could bring to light? She sighed, hoping to know in her spirit whether this was the Lord's making or some strange thing conceived out of a desperate mind.

Since the dinner, Beth and John had not spoken, despite the meetings he had with Mark to discuss the journey. Beth immersed herself in gathering what provisions the family would need to make the journey. They could take little with them but the necessities of life. Fingering her mother's tapestry inside the chest, Beth wondered what to do with it. Perhaps Mistress Worthington would keep watch over it here at the tavern during their absence. Besides her father's journal, it was the one material item she and her sister had that reminded them of their beloved parents, now gone. She hoped it would be safe.

Beth looked up at that moment, thinking of her parents and of Judith's confidence in the idea that, perhaps, they had relatives living somewhere in this new land. If they did find relatives from long ago, how would they make their acquaintance? Beth sighed. There was little use in pondering such things until the time came. For now, there was the journey to the place by the ocean that John Harris had described—with a sandy coastline stretching for eternity, accompanied by the laughter of the gulls.

Beth was closing the lid to the chest when suddenly she heard voices escalating in the room across the hall. She came out into the hallway and to the door, recognizing Mark's calm voice. The second voice belonged to an agitated man, the vexation clear in his words.

"Why must you do this?" the man demanded of her brother-in-law. "Now the entire expedition is in jeopardy!"

"I do what I believe is best. Surely you know we need them to help us carry our provisions. And they were most willing to do it for a few trinkets and gold coins."

"You don't understand, do you? You don't understand the danger in hiring people like them."

"There is danger in everything one does. But if we place our hope in Christ. . ."

"I have placed my hope in Christ, my lord. But living here in this place also calls for wisdom. And I can tell you there is no wisdom in hiring the heathen to do one's bidding. None whatsoever. There is only evil and a heavy price to pay."

Beth heard the sound of boots pounding across the wooden flooring.

"If you are determined to hire them, then I will not be re-sponsible for what happens on the journey. I cast the burden into your hands. You will take the risk. Not I."

"I'm more than willing to do so," said Mark. "I have no intention of putting any blame on you for whatever happens. 'Tis my choice alone."

"A choice at what cost? At the cost of the women's lives, for instance? Don't you know these people will kill and steal while you are looking the other way?"

"And have we not also done the same, Master Harris? Truly we have done our share of evil when we came to colonize this land, taking at will their lands without treaty, stealing what belongs to them, making off with food and other sundries."

Suddenly there came a growl, like some living animal of the night, just beyond the door. A chill swept through Beth. She glanced down to find her hands were shaking. Quickly she turned and began stepping back toward her room.

"So you make excuses for their massacres." John Harris spit the words, his voice seething. "Then we have no reason to do any further business. I relinquish my duties as guide. And I do pray you will open your eyes, my lord, and see that I'm right before it's too late."

Beth heard the latch to the other door rise. She hurried inside her room and closed her door, just as the men entered the hall.

"Master Harris, I beg you to reconsider. You know the very land we seek. I'm not certain what it is about the naturals that distresses you, but I believe God's hand is upon us. I know you can lead us there safely."

"I can't bear the responsibility if you insist on hiring them."

She heard the thump of footsteps. Peeking out the door, she caught a fleeting glimpse of John Harris as he escaped down the flight of stairs. Looking back, she found the grim face of Mark, and his sad eyes suddenly rested on her. "You overheard?"

"Yes. I don't understand. What happened with Mr. Harris?"

Mark sighed. "He and I do not agree about the naturals I

hired to help us with the journey. I found two Indians today willing to be porters for a price. But when I mentioned my intention to Master Harris, he became angry, insisting I was a fool and calling the naturals 'murdering heathen.' "

Beth's gaze fell once more on the stairs where John had disappeared.

"I don't know what to do," Mark said helplessly. "We need him to guide us to Hatorask. Without him, we can't go."

Beth wondered if Mark was waiting for her to come up with some manner of agreement between them. Nothing came to mind.

He turned on his heel, his head hanging low, and wandered off to the room in which the two men had quarreled, presumably to ponder the events that had just transpired. Beth considered what had happened. Perhaps God was at work through these circumstances by having John Harris refuse to lead them. Maybe they would have met danger had they gone, and John's wrath kept them from making an unwise decision. But then, she considered the words John uttered in their previous meetings. His obvious interest in the land of Hatorask. And his words of comfort, how he would protect her with his life and lead them all to safety. Why then had he chosen to abandon the journey? And why did he hate the Indians?

Beth returned to her room and sat down by her chest. She opened it to gaze once more at the tapestry and the bit of cheerful scenery on the material's surface. It was not a cheerful scene that came to her now but a flood of memories from a sadder time. In them she could still hear Father's angry outbursts that became more frequent as his illness progressed.

"I will not do business with the likes of that man!" his

voice roared. "He is out to kill me! Quick, bring the sword. I will deal with him. He will not live to see the sunrise!"

Somehow, Father had found a saber and begun waving it in the air. It chopped a chunk of wood out of a fine chair. Beth stared in horror at the sight. Her father, once noble and wise, now appeared an armed madman with his senses abandoned. *What can I do? Dear God, please help me!*

"Find him!" Father continued to shout. "I will cut him to pieces. I will tell him who it is that refuses to deliver Briarwood to him! Scoundrel!"

The tirade went on. All the servants went into hiding. No one knew what to do. Her father held them at bay with the anger of a depraved mind and a rapier in his hand.

Finally Beth burst into tears and begged him, "Father, please! Please put down your sword before we're all hurt!"

His anger ceased like a candle extinguished. The sword clattered to the ground, and with it her father, crumpled up on the floor, weeping, too exhausted to be moved.

Beth snapped her eyes open, realizing she had been dreaming. But it seemed real—as real as anything—as real as the encounter between John Harris and Mark. She began to shiver. All the fine words John had spoken, of protection and honor, seemed moot after this latest confrontation. She wanted to weep once more. There was no love in her future. No hope. She tried to shift her thoughts to things more pleasant but saw only anger and discontent.

Not long after, she met Judith in the hall. A look of sadness distorted her sister's otherwise chiseled features of firm, pale skin, tight cheeks, and a strong chin. "Judith? What ails you?"

She sighed. "Your wish has come true, Beth, and you had nothing to do with it."

"What wish is this?"

"Your wish not to go to Hatorask. Haven't you heard the news? There is no guide. John Harris's services are no longer at our disposal."

Beth bent her head and nodded. "I'm afraid I heard everything. I witnessed the conversation between Mr. Harris and your husband. Though I shouldn't have. . . ," she added hastily.

Judith drew closer, her eyebrows furrowed. "Please, tell me what was said. Why did this happen? Why is Mr. Harris no longer our guide?"

"Because your husband hired Indians to help us. John doesn't trust them. When Mark tried to reason with him, John told him he would not help, that he could not be held responsible should anything go ill. After that, he told Mark he would no longer be our guide."

Judith sighed. "Beth, you must go and confront Mr. Harris. Only you can reason with him."

Beth started, confused. "What? Why must I be the one to confront him?"

"Because he holds a great fondness for you. Everyone noticed it at dinner the other night. Surely you can change his heart."

Beth began to pace. "How can I trust myself to another angry man?" Suddenly all the pain of her father's care came rising to her lips in a tumult. "You were not there, Judith. You didn't see Father's tirades. Waving his sword, ready to cut us to pieces. Shouting to the bell tower itself. And there I was, trying to calm a tide worse than what the ocean can stir in a storm. I can't do that again. I don't know this man or what his temper can do. Yes, he was a gentleman at dinner, but after what I witnessed, I no longer know. . ."

Judith stood still and silent, observing her. Nothing was

said for several long moments. Then she sighed and nodded. "I do understand what you are saying, my sister. And it's true; we don't know what lies in his heart. All the more reason not to judge him so hastily until we do. And so you must find out. If not, our cause is lost."

"But why must it be me? Why can't you and Mark confront Mr. Harris? This is your dream, not mine."

Judith opened her mouth to reply, then shut it in haste. Again, several quiet moments slipped away, agonizing moments of silence. With it, Beth saw the relationship with her sister begin to slip, too. Would she allow her feelings and the past to destroy her last living relationship with a family member?

"I think it's plain to see why only you can do this. Mr. Harris has taken an obvious liking to you. You can see it in his eyes and hear it in his voice. I think if you go to him and implore him to change his mind, he will do so on your account."

"But what if this may be God's way of revealing His will? That we need to remain in the safety of Jamestown? That we may be placed in mortal danger if we go?"

"I don't believe that's true. Think of Father. The words he wrote. The longing in them. And somewhere deep inside of you, isn't there a longing, too? To know what happened to our family? To wonder if we are truly alone or if others exist? Ask yourself this, Beth. Seek out your true heart and see what it says."

Seek out my heart when right now my heart doesn't know what to believe? At first Beth had thought the whole venture foolish. Then she saw with her own eyes Father's writings, before the madness overcame him and the true reality of the world left him. He talked of seeking the truth about the colony at Roanoke and his parents' whereabouts. Then came the memory of John's words—the description of this land of Hatorask, of windswept beaches, seabirds, the ocean, and land unfettered by the growing masses, ready to be claimed for the Lord. She considered all these things, comparing them with what lay in her heart. *Not my will, but Thine be done, Lord. Guide me and lead me for Thy name's sake.*

Beth spent the afternoon by the river James. She watched the ripples on the water fanned to life by a steady breeze. At that moment, she desired a change in her life. Since coming to this land, fear ruled everything. Now she earnestly wanted to do away with such feelings and stand firm and decisive. She did not want to be that ocean wave talked about in the book of James, tossed back and forth, full of doubt. She wanted to step forward in faith, just as her grandparents had done when they embarked on that fateful journey long ago, not knowing what would happen. They likely had fears, as well. . .fears that they might not survive the journey by sea. Or when they arrived, fears of the new land and the new inhabitants they faced. But somehow they had overcome them to be a part of the colony. Wasn't their fortitude embedded in her, their granddaughter? At least she had picked up roots and come here. She had begun the walk. Now it was time to continue the journey. And the only way she could find out if her road led to Hatorask was to talk with John Harris.

Beth stood to her feet, whispering a prayer, hoping for God's grace and guidance. It seemed ironic that she would be the one to try and convince John to lead the expedition, but such was the leading of God in these matters. In His will she must trust.

She had not gone far when she discovered John Harris

in the main thoroughfare leading to Jamestown, conversing with another man. They talked boisterously as if they knew each other. She heard a brief mention of the Indians.

"And that's the way it's going to be, Samuel," John said sternly.

"You're a fool, John Harris. You can't let the past do this to you."

"This is not foolishness but wisdom. How else does one plan for the future without learning the lessons of the past?"

John turned then, just as she approached. Their eyes met. Suddenly Beth was overcome with timidity. She withdrew, turning aside and striding for the opposite end of the street. Despite her willingness, she didn't have the confidence to confront him, not with his anger still so fresh.

Suddenly she heard her name. "Miss Colman! Beth! Please wait!"

Somehow she managed to stop. He came forward, hesitant himself, his eyes wide with obvious concern. "You overheard?"

"I did not mean to pry, Mr. Harris. I was planning to meet you, but the occasion doesn't present itself to a friendly meeting."

"Please don't think wrong of me." He paused. "I—I didn't want you to hear."

"But I have, Mr. Harris. I've heard everything."

He appeared startled. "What do you mean?"

"I overheard the conversation at the tavern with my brother-in-law. Who couldn't help but hear your angry words? I know all about anger, you see. I saw it every day in my father. And I must say I'm glad you won't be our guide. I couldn't bear to come under it all again." She began to walk away, only to sense his presence behind her, confirmed by the sound of his footsteps.

"Please don't leave like this. I wish I could make you understand."

"Then why don't you?"

He shook his head. "There are some things that must be put aside for another time and place."

"Then we have nothing more to discuss." Again she began to withdraw, and again he followed her like a shadow cast upon the ground. She turned. "Mr. Harris? Why are you following me?"

"Please, let me make amends. I don't want you distressed over this." He sighed. " 'Twas wrong of me to say what I did to your brother-in-law. Surely you can forgive me as our Savior Christ has done, as He implores us to do even now, when we have been wronged. Even to seventy times seven."

Beth could see his internal pain in the way his forehead crinkled and the tense lines that ran across his face.

"If it will help, I will go right this moment and ask your brother-in-law for his forgiveness." His expression seemed to say—*I will do all that and more, only please don't be unhappy with me.*

Beth sighed. "Do whatever you feel you must, Mr. Harris."

He said no more but left with only a cloud of dust in his wake. She shook her head, wondering more and more about this man. He held to some deep-seated unhappiness within, especially where the naturals of the land were concerned. Though she did want to know where it came from, she feared the answer. And yet he was willing to relinquish everything, for her sake. That spoke a far greater volume than any angry words.

❧

Later, as Beth was sitting down to do some mending, Judith hurried in, her face all aglow.

"Oh, Beth! Whatever did you say to make him change his mind?"

She glanced up, startled by the greeting. "I don't understand."

"Mr. Harris, of course. He went and told Mark how wrong he was, that Mark could hire whomever he chose, but that he would be most humble to accept the position of a guide if Mark would agree to take him back. Oh, 'tis a miracle from on high!"

Beth stared, dumbfounded. "I said practically nothing," she admitted. "I did mention Father and his periods of anger. I told him I was glad he wasn't our guide." She chuckled. "As if that would make him change his mind!"

Judith marveled. "Whatever you said, he did change his mind. God was with you." She embraced her. "Oh Beth, you don't know how happy this makes me."

Beth was glad for her sister's joy but could only wonder if she'd done the right thing and what would come of it all in the end—especially where she and John Harris were concerned.

five

He had been fool, just as Samuel had said. Blind and deaf, too, but certainly not dumb, for he had spoken his mind openly. He had unleashed his tongue like some venomous serpent insofar as what the lovely Beth Colman had witnessed at the tavern. If only he had known she was nearby when he spouted the angry words to Mark Reynolds. He would have bitten his tongue, swallowed down his indignation, and refused to allow the past to grip his actions. Now it was too late.

John sighed. How he wished Mark hadn't hired Indians, but the man felt he was doing what was right. Mark had no notion of the past. John should have realized it from the start and not cast his discontent upon the man. And certainly he would have never lashed out had he realized Beth was in the other room. Now she had witnessed an angry man, unable to bridle his tongue, full of vengeance and hate, a grim reminder of her past.

If only I could take it back. I'd tear up every word. Or better yet, cast it into the fire. He felt no better after confronting Mark, offering the sincerest of apologies and grateful that the man had reinstated him to the position of guide. But it was Beth's reaction—her wide brown eyes and drawn face—that marked his dreams at night. Her unhappiness with him. Her sadness the day when they met by the river. He must bring himself back into her good graces, but how? Soon they would be leaving for the southern regions. The

49

possessions were all but ready. He had seen the Indians
Mark hired, hovering near the tavern, though John tried
his best not to think about them. He had met with Mark
once more to discuss the route of their journey by way of a
crude map. But he did not feel right beginning this venture
without restoring Beth's confidence in him. The idea that he
would protect her and give her honor, as he once told her at
the dinner table, seemed fruitless unless this changed. He
wanted her to cling to his promise of safety. To trust him.
To cleave to him, especially as they began this trek into
unpredictable regions. But first he must mend the breach.

"You're looking quite sad again," commented his friend
Samuel. John looked up from the small stick he had been
whittling, even as his mind sorted through these myriad
thoughts. "I thought you would be in good spirits, now that
you have rejoined the journey to Hatorask. What is ailing
you this time?"

John wanted to convey the situation to Samuel but feared
the man might scorn his reasoning. . .or ask once more when
he planned to resolve the past that still dictated his actions.

"You have made peace concerning the naturals that are
coming on the journey, yes?"

John shrugged. "As much peace as one can muster, considering the circumstances."

"Then is it the woman you prefer?"

He stepped back, amazed by the man's perception. "How
did you know? Is it that obvious?"

Samuel laughed. "I have eyes, my friend. It isn't hard to
see. I always believed you should find a good woman and
settle down. You need to put aside that restless nature of
yours. You have found such a woman, haven't you?"

"The sister-in-law of the man who hired me to guide

them. But she no longer accepts me."

"What have you done?"

He twisted his lips. "Need I say? You know about the confrontation I had with Master Reynolds concerning the Indians. She overheard me speak about it and in a tongue not in keeping with a gentleman, I fear."

"Ah. So now she thinks you're some untamed beast."

"Or worse. What shall I do?"

"Have you told her about the past?"

He shook his head. "I can't burden her with my troubles."

"But it seems you already have. No doubt she knows that some unrest lurks in you. You will have to tell her."

John shook his head. "I refuse to speak about it. You know it, of course. To do so again would open the wounds."

Samuel plunked himself down on a rocky boulder beside John. "My friend, you must show her you're not a man of stone but one with a cheerful countenance, able to defend her and help her. You can be cheerful, yes?"

"When I'm with her, I am." John sighed once more. He felt renewed around Beth as if he were embracing the warm wind, flying high like one of the gulls that soared above the shores of Hatorask.

"Then go to her. Charm her. Convince her there is nothing to fear concerning you, that you made a mistake. Assure her it will not happen again." He nodded at the tiny cross John had whittled. "You may even yet hold the key in your hand."

John looked at the cross and grinned. "I cling to this more now than ever, I must say. Though I can do without its suffering. 'Tis too heavy a burden for any soul to bear."

"But Christ bore it for you. You needn't keep bearing it." Samuel nodded. "You will one day need to reconcile the past,

John. 'Tis the only way there will be light for the future. You have seen for yourself what the past can do."

Oh, to reconcile the past. To have that peace that surpasses all understanding. Yes, it would be good to sit beside Beth, stare into her lovely eyes, and confess to her all the trouble he carried. But he could envision the look as she thought of her own pain concerning the deaths in her family and her father. Maybe she didn't wish to revel in further sorrow. How could he inflict more on her than what she had already endured? No, he couldn't tell her. Not now. He vowed before God to restrain his grief, to keep hidden his past, to allow God Himself to rectify the situation. It must be this way.

Looking at the cross, he found a piece of leather twine and looped it through the small hole he had made at the top. A crude type of jewelry, in a way, but symbolizing much power. Perhaps Beth would accept the gift as a peace offering and, in turn, change her opinion of him. He'd found her of interest from the moment he laid eyes on her, looking lost and in need of a friend. And he wanted to be that friend, that confidant—the one who would supply every need, if he did not allow his own needs to overshadow all else.

John stood to his feet, holding the cross, walking the length of the road to see that another ship had come to port. From the shallop came more women, looking as fearful and uncertain as Beth had the day she arrived. But none of them matched her beauty or her spirit, even as he saw them cling to their belongings, searching around, hoping for a friendly face. At one time, he might have been there to help them, looking for that special woman with whom he could set up a home. Instead, he would travel to Hatorask, perhaps with the very woman he would one day marry. That is, if God opened the door between them that had been shut tight by his heedless actions.

Wandering back to the Worthington Tavern, he found Master and Mistress Reynolds lingering in the main room, organizing their meager belongings for the trip. Both of them looked up and smiled when he entered, as if they were pleased to see him.

"Are we soon ready to depart for the southern region, Master Harris?" Mark inquired.

"Very soon. 'Tis a pleasant time to travel. In the summer there are known to be fierce windstorms and wicked heat." He glanced around, hoping to find the delicate form of Beth thereabouts, but caught no glimpse of her. He panicked. Had she decided not to be a part of the expedition after all? Had she turned aside from him and embraced another life? "Pray tell, where is Miss Colman? She isn't ill, is she?"

Mark and Judith exchanged glances. "Not at all," Mark said. "She is quite well."

He hesitated, wondering how he should broach the subject of a meeting with her before their journey commenced. He felt the cross he had whittled, nestled in the palm of his hand. The key, as Samuel had called it, and one he prayed would unlock her heart. "I—I have something I would like to give her."

"I can call for her," Judith announced, hurrying to the stairs. John said nothing, even though he could sense Mark's questioning glance, wondering what might be happening. He did not wish for another confrontation with the man but ignored his inquiry to think of the meeting to come.

After a time, John heard footsteps on the stairs. Beth Colman appeared, as radiant as always, dressed in a colorful gown of forest green and a shawl about her shoulders. She did not look him in the eye but stared at the floor. "Yes, Mr. Harris?"

He drew in a sharp breath. How would he begin, and with Judith and Mark watching? "I have something to show you, Miss Colman. Something I believe will put to rest all your questions."

Her gaze lifted to meet his. Her eyebrows narrowed. "I have no more questions, Mr. Harris. You have answered them all."

He swallowed hard, wondering what she meant. Could it be the meeting the other day proved more fearsome than he imagined—that he was to her a crazed man like her father, controlled by anger and without the cheerfulness that could win her heart?

"Dear Beth," Judith admonished, "go with Mr. Harris and see what he is offering. All of our work here is finished. We have time. You have not been to the river today. You like it so well, and 'tis a fine day for a walk."

"I would be glad to accompany you to the river," John quickly offered, trying not to sound too eager. Inwardly he wanted to thank Mark's wife for the suggestion.

Beth hesitated. He waited for what seemed like a long time. Finally she nodded, much to his relief. John escorted her out into the bright sunshine. She kept her gaze averted, concentrating instead on her surroundings as if taking it all in, piece by piece. At the river there were children playing and a few women doing the wash. They both meandered farther upstream. No words came to his mind. Instead, they walked until they came to an area filled with blooming flowers. Here Beth stopped. A smile lit her face.

"How lovely," she cooed, picking a flower. "There are no such flowers like these in England. I wonder what they are."

"I'm not certain, madam." He picked one flower with a particularly large golden head, turned upward as if poised to drink of the sun's rays. "This looks much like a china cup in its saucer, ready for tea."

Beth laughed. The tension began to melt away. "It does indeed. Are there flowers like these at Hatorask?"

"Along the shores, the tall grasses sometimes put forth heads that look as if they could be flowers. But I've seen pointed plants that sometimes send up flowers in a straight stalk. The tips of the leaves are sharp and can cut like a knife."

She stood perfectly still, seeming to absorb every word he spoke. "A leaf of a plant as sharp as a knife?"

He nodded. "Look in the woods about you, and you will find other flowering trees as well."

Beth slowly sank into the patch of flowers. "Why does such a place like Hatorask intrigue you, Mr. Harris? 'Tis because of these things you've described?"

"Hatorask is unlike any place I have ever seen. The land by the ocean has its own way about it. And, I suppose, without any settlements, it seems very new, like the hand of God just created it. There are long stretches of untouched sands as far as the eye can see. Tall grasses. The never-ending sound of the ocean speaking. Even shells where one can hear the echo of the ocean."

Beth straightened. "How I would love to see and hear all this!"

John smiled, feeling as if he were beginning to draw her heart unto his. "There are islands as well, surrounded by waters. Small bits of land allow one to cross here and there by boat. You need a boat to see much of it. One could live on an island and feel separated from the world."

"I don't know if I would want to live like that," she said. "People need people. To be so isolated. . .where do you worship God? Or trade for supplies?"

"One can worship God in any place. Where two or more are gathered, He is there with them."

"I suppose." She plucked several more flowering teacups. "This will make a fine bouquet to give to Judith." She paused. "So what concerns you about the Indians, Mr. Harris?"

The suddenness of her question took him by surprise. "Please believe me when I say 'tis of no further concern, Miss Colman."

"There must be some reason why you have such strong feelings on the matter." She glanced at him out of the corner of her eye.

"I was hasty and judgmental, seeking only my needs and not the needs of others. I hope you will forgive me as your brother-in-law has done."

"Of course. I only thought. . ." She paused. "Sometimes 'tis good to speak of one's ills."

If only he could. But it would be too difficult. And he refused to shed tears before her, to show any sign of weakness when he must be strong and capable with the journey close at hand. "A friend I think of as a brother knows everything. I have confessed to him so I might find healing."

"I see. I only hope you realize that I too have been through much concerning my father. I can provide a listening ear whenever you wish."

"I will remember that, Beth. I mean, Miss Colman."

"You may call me Beth. At least 'tis better than Elizabeth. Imagine being named after the queen of England from long ago." She chuckled. "I do hope I don't carry the stigma of being unmarried, like our virgin queen."

John stared, unable to believe what he was hearing. After all that had occurred, he felt certain Beth would spurn him. Let him go. Have nothing more to do with an angry man such as himself. And here she was, plainly talking about marriage as if she were considering it.

"Not that I mean to hint—" she added hastily, her cheeks all aflame.

"Of course. Though I'm certain a woman of your virtue does consider such a union from time to time."

"And do you, Mr. Harris? Or do you seek only to explore and conquer a new land?"

He couldn't tell if she was exploring the new land of a relationship by way of these questions or simply looking for honest communication. "I open myself to whatever the Lord wills for my life. And it appears His will right now is to lead you and your family safely to Hatorask."

Beth nodded and gathered the flowers she had picked. "A wise answer," she mused. "We are two of a kind, don't you agree, Mr. Harris?"

"That remains to be seen, Miss Colman. I mean, Beth. But I would say we are indeed on a path of mutual understanding and maybe admiration, as well."

Her face grew even rosier. He escorted her back to the tavern, wishing her a good day before a sigh of blessed relief escaped. The meeting had gone far better than any dream he could have mustered. Just then, he opened his hand and saw the small cross he had whittled. And he had not even given her the gift he'd promised! John closed his hand over the precious item. But God had done so much more. He would save the cross for some time in the future, he decided. A time when it would mean the most to the both of them. Maybe even on the day he asked for her hand in marriage. . .as a symbol of an everlasting covenant. *May it be Your will, Lord, and in Your time.*

᪥

On the day of their departure from Jamestown, John witnessed a new and vibrant Beth Colman standing by her family, ready to embark on this latest adventure. He took little notice of the Indians ready to serve as bearers for the company's belongings. He kept his sights trained on Beth, who appeared radiant in the morning light, wearing a slight smile on her lips.

"Are we ready to depart for Hatorask, Master Harris?" Mark inquired.

"Yes, my lord. 'Tis a fine day for travel. I have never seen the sky so blue. . . ." *Or Beth looking so radiant.* He forced the thought away to concentrate on the tasks before him. He must give all his attention to the matter at hand, knowing there would be many quiet moments in which to reflect on the woman who had all but captured his heart.

Mark Reynolds knelt in the dirt, bowed his head, and offered up a prayer for their journey. John listened carefully to the man's humble prayer. At once, he sensed peace for the venture. "Guide us in Thy heavenly light, O Lord," Mark prayed. "Preserve us by Thy mighty hand. Keep us in Thy tender mercies, we pray. And reveal to us the mystery from the past ages through Thy wisdom, the mystery of our family, long since parted from us."

When the prayer had concluded, Mark slowly stood to his feet, a smile on his face. "We are ready."

Are you ready as well, John Harris? came a quiet voice within his spirit. John arranged the two sacks he had slung over each shoulder and felt for the snaphaunce pistol tucked in a leather strap about his waist. *Not by your might or your power, but only by His spirit, John Harris. Remember that, lest you forget and you find yourself on a journey of no return.*

six

Slap!

Her hand went for the whining mosquito that hovered over her arm, ready to embed itself in her flesh. Again she slapped at it, managing to crush the tiny menace beneath her fingers, finding a trickle of blood in its wake. *How dreadful,* Beth mourned, taking out a bit of cloth to wipe the dampness from her face. Never had she witnessed such warmth nor seen so many of these mosquitoes that bit her exposed flesh. She couldn't recall a day like this in England. Then again, it was rare she found herself in tall grasses, walking for any great distance. In England, only the cold walls of Briarwood surrounded her, the stillness broken by Father's moans for help. After slapping her arm when she again felt an annoying bite, she had to wonder if that time spent at Briarwood was any more dreadful than what she'd been experiencing here these last ten days.

"Try this salve, madam," John offered, holding out a small flask. "It will help keep them from biting."

"This is terrible," Beth complained, smearing the foul-smelling grease on her hands and arms. "Why is there such a plague here?"

" 'Tis very warm for this time of year," he admitted. "The sun has driven them out of the swamps. Usually there are no such swarms until later in May."

Beth watched another of the biting mosquitoes. It flew above her skin as if examining the strange oily substance she had smeared on before it decided to find a tasty morsel elsewhere. "I've never seen such land, either," she remarked, again patting her forehead with a handkerchief. "There is so much water. My feet are very wet. I don't think I've ever had wet feet like this. I'm afraid my shoes will never hold together." She gazed upward, allowing the breezes to sweep across her flushed face, providing a cool respite from the hot day. "I smell salt. Or fish, perhaps."

" 'Tis the swampland filled with water from the ocean. The land here is quite low. When the oceans rise in a storm, water flows upriver, bringing with it the creatures of the sea."

What a strange land this was, this Virginia, or now this province of Carolana, as John called it. Beth had already witnessed a few large flying seabirds that John pointed out. One had huge wings and a long, pointed beak. John said the beak was used to grab fish from the sea for the bird's dinner. Despite the swarms of mosquitoes, the heat, and the dampness, Beth had to admit she was learning something new each day, even if the circumstances were difficult. There was a certain joy to be found in a new and different place. The Lord God had made it all, both the good and the bad.

When he mentioned the ocean, she asked how far away it was.

"Well, if one goes east," he said, pointing, "one would see the beginnings of the ocean in a few hours."

"Then we must go at once!" Beth announced, lifting her skirts, ready to see the spectacle so described to her in the conversations of late. It would be grand to see the white sandy beaches and the ocean tides sweeping the shore. She could hardly wait.

John laughed. "We are not going that way, madam. Patience. There is plenty of time. When we reach Hatorask, there will be ocean waters as far as you can see. You will have no want of it. None at all." He paused. "So tell me about your home in England."

"Surely you remember our mother country."

"I lived by the sea. I never traveled to the interior regions. Only to London on occasion, to engage in business for my father. He was a fisherman by trade."

Beth turned, suddenly curious. It was the first time he had spoken about his family.

"Why do you look at me so?"

"I only thought perhaps you might be an orphan. I've never heard you talk about your family."

He shrugged. "They remain in England. I've not heard from them in a very long time." He paused as if ready to say something else, but instead said, "Tell me about your home. Where in England did you dwell?"

"In Cambridge, a small town with many fine dwellings and great men of wisdom, it seems. My father gained his title by birthright. Our manor was Briarwood. A fine home with many beautiful gardens. Mother loved her gardens, and I suppose I did as well."

"I saw your interest in the flowers by the river James where we spoke," he commented. "There are many flowers here in the land, as well as flowering trees. Many things exist here that one doesn't see in England. Animals also."

"Besides the seabirds with the long beaks?"

He chuckled. "In fact, there is a strange animal here that washes its food in the water. I saw it one evening by the river James."

Beth halted, even as the party consisting of her sister, brother-in-law, and the Indians disappeared through a bank of thick rushes. "An animal that cleans its food? I've never heard of such a thing."

"A furry little animal, about this big." John spanned the width with his hands. "It has thick fur, useful for many things." He then circled his eyes with his fingers.

Beth laughed at his antics. "Why do you do that?"

"Because the animal has large, black circles around its eyes."

"I only remember the black circle Father once had around his eye when he fell and hit his face," Beth recalled. "I don't think I've ever seen an animal like that."

"The heathen. . .that is, the Indians call them *aroughcuns*. They are native to this land. Maybe we will see one if we come upon some fresh water at our camp. They like to roam about at night and sleep during the day."

She laughed. "I must say, all this conversation regarding some black-eyed animal has me wondering what other surprises lay ahead on this journey."

He winked. "There could be a great many. One never knows."

Beth tried to imagine such a creature, even as she gazed about to find that her brother-in-law and sister had vanished, along with the Indians. How she wanted to share with them this new discovery, like so many she was making in the heart of a new land. "I wonder where Judith and her husband are. I must tell them about this aroughcun." She hurried a few paces, calling for them. Only the sound of the wind met her ears. "Where could they be?"

John said nothing, his cheerful countenance suddenly replaced by narrow eyes and tightness around his mouth. Beth tried not to come to any conclusions, but the look he gave concerned her. They hurried through the reeds, even as John called loudly for Mark.

"I'm sure they are fine. . . ," Beth began. Instead she found herself trying to keep up with John, who began to run, his hands batting away the foliage. Something possessed his steps, an urgency that sent fear welling up within her. "Mr. Harris. . .John. . .please wait. I'm sure they haven't gone far. We were talking for a time. They must have gone on ahead."

He only looked wildly around. "I knew this would happen. I said as much. But your brother-in-law chose not to heed me."

Beth panted, even as she drew close to him. "W—what?" she inquired breathlessly, trying to wipe away the dampness collecting on her forehead before it stung her eyes with its salty touch.

"I knew trouble would arise with these heathen when our backs were turned. He would not listen. He is as obstinate as any I have ever met."

Beth stared. "I don't understand."

"They are evil! I warned Master Reynolds with every part of my being, but would he listen? No!"

She gasped. "John, don't say such things! Th—they are fine. I'm certain of it." But doubt began to creep up alongside the fear and made a combination that nearly paralyzed her. *Please help us, dear Lord!*

"Hurry, we waste time!" John urged, taking her by the hand. They traveled what seemed a very long time, though Beth didn't know how far. Her legs began to grow heavy. Her parched throat begged for a few droplets of water.

"They are deceptive, wily. We only stopped for a moment, but a moment is all they need." He swept his face with his hand. "Why did this have to happen, Lord?"

Suddenly they heard the sound of exclamation. Beth turned and found a small rise of land, and standing on it were Judith and Mark. They waved at them. Beth hurried forward with John close behind.

"Come see!" Judith exclaimed. " 'Tis not much, I know, but we can see a little bit of the lay of the land."

Beth instead ran up and clung to her sister as if she would never let go. "We were so worried, Judith! We stopped to talk, and then I couldn't find you."

"There's no reason to fear, sister. The Indians communicated to us this lookout. I needed a bit of rest after the long walk. 'Tis quite warm today. And while we were here, they found us water to drink."

Beth couldn't believe how cheerful Judith was, even after what she had been through. Looking back at John, she saw the reddish hue of anger begin to seep across his face. He was staring at the Indians, who pointed to themselves and then to the white people in their presence.

"I will not be made a fool again," he snarled at them. "I know what you're planning. I have my eye on you, to be sure." He withdrew his pistol.

Both the Indians grew rigid. They made loud sounds, pointing to the weapon, and from what Beth could discern, uttered the words *fire stick*.

"Master Harris, what are you doing?" Mark exclaimed, holding out his hand. "Put that away."

"I told you they couldn't be trusted. You chose not to listen."

"They guided us to this place and then went to find us fresh water. There is no cause for this. They are only doing what I hired them to do. They mean us no harm."

"They are sneaky and deceptive. What will it take to convince you, my lord? You need to understand, once and for all, that they can't be trusted."

"Or is it you that can't be trusted with other living souls, John Harris? Let us be honest, for they have done nothing on this journey to betray your trust."

John whirled, his eyes widening, as if the words hurt him more than if Mark had struck his face. Beth closed her eyes, praying against another altercation between John and Mark. When she opened them, John had vanished. Her feet shifted, ready to follow him. Instead, she felt the firm hand of Mark on her arm. "Let him alone, Beth."

"I wish I knew what troubled him," Beth murmured with a sigh. "He refuses to say. Whatever it is runs deep, so deep no one can find it, maybe not even John himself."

"Only God can give him the strength to face it," Mark said. "We can't do it alone. And you mustn't think this is your quest to help him, Beth. You will only find yourself swept away by it. All you can do is pray for him."

How much she needed to pray, more than ever. She paused to consider the many prayers offered up while she cared for Father and the way her strength nearly gave out by tending to his needs night and day. Only when she spoke to a caring minister, who came one day to Briarwood, did she find her strength renewed. He told her, as Mark had done now, not to carry the burden of her father's illness. She must cast it upon the Lord and allow His strength to sustain her. After that, she felt the weight fall from her heavily laden shoulders and found the ability to face a new sunrise. And likewise, she would be able to face the sunrise of each new day here in this land, praying and hoping that the burden would soon be lifted from John. When that happened, perhaps they might embrace a future together, if God be willing.

Some time passed before John finally returned. He said nothing, not even acknowledging her, but pointed the way back to the original path and their journey southward to the land of Hatorask. Beth tried to quell the disappointment that rose up within. They had been having such a pleasant day, too, except for the biting mosquitoes and the warmth that even now renewed the dampness on the back of her neck. How she wished he would reveal more about this land, but in particular, more about himself. If nothing else, there was one thing she realized in light of all this. Somehow, the Indians had wounded his soul, and one day he would have to reconcile the cause of his pain.

When the sun began to dip low in the horizon, they stopped to make camp. As usual, John went seeking stout evergreen boughs with which to build a shelter for her and Judith. Beth did what she could with Judith to help prepare some kind of meal for them. The Indians had taught them how to bake corncakes on a stone in the fire. This and whatever meat the men were able to procure became their evening meal and their morning victual. Beth immediately set to work grinding corn kernels into meal while Judith fetched water. Beth had hardly worked with food back in England, as the servants did most of the cooking. She found the chore tiresome but worthwhile, especially the first time she made the corncakes. John had given her a smile, telling her how wonderful they were—much better than anything Mistress Worthington at the tavern could make. But now she didn't see him about, even as she began mixing the batter. She wished she could see the twinkle in his blue eyes and the smile that warmed her more than any blazing fire.

"It will be well with us," Judith tried to reassure her.

"I only wish it would be well with Mr. Harris," Beth murmured. "You don't think he will use his pistol against the Indians?"

"Oh, Beth, I pray not." She hesitated. "Have you talked to him about his anger?"

"I have asked, but he refuses to say. 'Tis painful for him. I wish he would talk about it. Maybe he believes we will think ill of him if he does. A matter of pride." Beth formed the cakes between her hands, putting them at once on the hot stone in the middle of the fire pit. She wiped away the dampness on her face. "Someone has to break through to his heart, or he will never be able to give his heart away to anyone."

Judith gave her a knowing nod. They finished their work in silence. When the cakes were done, the men returned empty-handed from their hunting venture. The cakes would be their meal. They ate quietly. The Indians sat off by themselves, saying little, though Beth could see how they stared at John with a certain trepidation outlined in their black eyes. *God, please bring Your peace to this place and to John's heart.*

Just then his voice broke the silence. "In two days we'll camp in sight of the ocean."

The announcement took them all by surprise. "I thought we still had quite a journey left," Mark said.

"We'll need another day on land, and then we'll need canoes for the crossing to Roanoke Island."

"Will there be canoes waiting for us?" Mark wondered.

"If there are none left from other explorers, we can make them," John told them confidently before taking another bite of the cake Beth had made.

Beth could not comprehend how one made a boat seaworthy enough to cross some wild ocean to another land. When he explained how the water in the sound was a mere third of a fathom deep and without waves, she rested a bit easier. At least they wouldn't be in some tiny little boat in a vast ocean, tossed here and there by the angry waves, perhaps even to be cast out to sea, forever lost in the powerful deep.

The crossing he described seemed easily done.

"Surely the naturals know how to make boats, as well," Mark commented.

Beth wondered how John would react upon the mention of the Indians. He only shrugged. "I'm certain they do."

She breathed a bit easier. Perhaps God had heard her prayer and brought peace to their camp. *Oh, may it be!*

Later that evening, as the sun made its departure, the western skies turned a dazzling red. Beth gazed at it for a time, marveling at the beauty, until she felt a presence draw near. She knew without a word it was John. She could sense his strength and purpose, despite the trouble he held within.

"May I sit with you?"

She nodded, and he took a seat beside her.

"You must see the sunrise over the ocean," he said, acknowledging the pretty sight before them. " 'Tis a wonder to behold. A giant red ball of light slowly rising out of the ocean depths."

Suddenly the words rushed out of her in a tumult. "You wouldn't have used your pistol on the Indians, would you, John? Would you have killed them?"

He turned in a start. "Beth. . ."

She continued to stare as the reddish haze began to fade, replaced by the shadows of night and the twinkling of the stars in the sky. "You frightened everyone. Is this the way it must be? Is there no other way?"

Silence met her earnest questioning. Doubts once more assailed her concerning this man and the shadow of his past that seemed to follow his every move.

"There are always other ways," he finally conceded. "I did what I did only out of necessity. An act of readiness, I suppose."

"Readiness for what? Do you truly think the naturals wish us harm?"

"I don't know. I pray not. I am concerned about what lies ahead. That your brother-in-law's fascination with finding out the truth about your relatives may be clouding his judgment. You truly don't understand the dangers that exist here. You must be on your guard at all times, lest you be caught unaware." He sighed. "That's why I don't sleep much at night. I keep awake to watch the camp and you. You all are my responsibility. And I won't fail, even if you don't understand or accept my actions."

"Then I guess we're truly blessed to have a man like you to protect us." She noticed the look of gratitude that filled his face.

"I'm very glad to hear you say that." He took her hand in his for a moment. "As I said in the tavern, I will do whatever I must to see that you're protected. With my life, if necessary. I give you my word."

She looked at his hand covering hers, a large hand, strong and able, with skin slightly weathered and tanned by the wind and sun. How could she doubt his sincerity? Even with the untold anger stowed away inside, he wished only to do good. And she would accept what he said and the hand that held hers, at least for now.

seven

Beth tried to keep her attention on her surroundings but couldn't help but be distracted by the stirring of the paddle and the one who commanded it with a firm grip. They sat facing each other in the canoe, John on one end, Judith on the other, while Beth occupied the center. She had thought of sitting in such a position as to keep her back to him as she had on previous crossings. Instead, this time when she came into the boat, she sat facing him. From that moment on, their eyes were locked in silent communion but for occasional glances at the scenery. She liked the way he commanded the paddle. His shirt billowed with the breezes off the bay, making the shirtsleeves appear like miniature sails. Back and forth his arms moved, drawing their canoe ever closer to the island chain he called Hatorask.

When they had first arrived at a place where they saw the coast of some distant land, John had let out a gleeful shout. It was unlike the other river crossings they had made where Beth thought the time had come for their arrival. From his reaction, Beth knew they had at last made it. He left them to explore the thick rushes by the water's edge, hoping to find some abandoned canoes. Again came his glee-filled shout. "God is with us," he declared. "There are several boats where others have left them. Praise be."

"Have many explored this region?" Mark inquired.

John nodded, describing how he once came as an explorer, too, not only to map the region, but for curiosity's sake. He admitted the draw of the famed lost colony also brought many others here, seeking their whereabouts. "You are not the first hoping to learn what happened to that colony," he said.

"Have you heard what others have found?" Mark asked.

"From what I've learned, the news is not good. Most believed they were massacred." John cast a glance toward their Indian companions, who were loading possessions into one of the canoes. "There are many unfriendly Indians in the region, particularly in the interior parts. But there were a few friendly souls among them. One, Manteo, befriended the colonists. He knew some English. In fact, I heard it said he even went to visit England."

Mark smiled. "Then there's hope."

John raised his eyebrow. "Hope, sir? We speak of a time sixty years past. People long since gone, if not killed, then dead from age or other circumstances, with their whereabouts unknown. It will be difficult if not impossible to find what you seek."

Mark appeared to pay John's words little mind. As Judith had so rightly observed, once his attention was engaged in a matter, he refused to be moved. Beth had to admire her brother-in-law's resolve in those instances. Up against such obstacles, most would grow weary and give up the quest. But Mark possessed a strength about him that Beth couldn't help but admire. How she prayed she would find a husband his equal, if not greater.

She now turned, watching John while he manned his post, even as his attention remained on the land mass that grew ever closer. Did he also have characteristics of strength and tenacity? He did traverse these places without fear. He had a determination back in Jamestown to come find others and seek reconciliation when things were amiss. These were all excellent qualities in a man. If only there were not the shadows of past events clouding it all.

"Are we soon upon Hatorask?" she inquired.

"This is all Hatorask. We go first to the island of Roanoke. 'Twas once called the city of Raleigh for the man who helped finance the colony. When I came here last, 'twas more a city of desolation."

"Are there any remains of the colony to be seen?" Judith asked.

"Only a little. Scavengers have devoured it. Not many clues linger."

Beth nearly chuckled. Such news would not dissuade Mark. He would inquire of God for clues and no doubt would find some. She sat up straighter as the vegetation became visible. Thick forests came into view but nothing of any settlements. No boats could be seen either but only the vast blue-gray waters before them. Just then, she caught sight of something darting in the water. The strange, large gray fish leaped into the air before burying itself once more in the ocean depths. Another followed suit. "Look at that! Up there!"

John turned. "Yes, I see them."

"What large fish!"

He laughed. "And strange fish they are, as well. They can jump quite far out of the water. And they blow water out of the tops of their heads."

Beth would have stood up were it not for John's hand on her arm, urging her to stay seated. The canoe pitched with her excitement. "Look! They seem to stare at us from out of the water, as if to inquire why we're here." She laughed in glee. John smiled, too, as if enjoying her discoveries. "I can't begin to think what else we might find in this place."

"One never knows," he admitted. "But I'm certain you will remember this time always."

Beth hoped to recall such things in her thoughts and her heart, even as the land suddenly came upon them. John guided the canoe to the sandy shore and promptly helped her and Judith to firm ground. "Welcome to Roanoke Island."

"So this is the place, my wife," Mark said expectantly. "The place where your grandparents once lived."

Beth gazed about at the trees swaying in the fine breeze. It seemed strange not to see a house or two. Everything appeared quiet and still but for the movement made by the play of wind upon the leaves. Following John, she brushed by rushes nearly as tall as she. Birds chirped from the trees. They had not gone far when Mark hailed a halt to the procession.

He knelt and picked up a hewn timber. "This was cut by an ax."

"We will find some remains of the colony," John admitted. "This may have been from a stockade they once built."

As they continued on, Mark found more evidence of habitation long since decayed by time and weather. More hewn timbers made by the tools of men. Beth was so intent on finding an artifact from long ago, she tripped over a rock and landed in some leaves. John was by her side at once, helping her to her feet. "Are you hurt?" he asked, picking out the leaves entangled in her hair.

"No. Thank you." She tried not to look at his face, even as steady warmth once more began to invade her cheeks. Peering instead at her feet, she then noticed the cause of her fall. It was not a rock but some round object, solid and black. "What could that be?"

Mark was at her side, picking up the heavy fragment. "This is made of iron," he said, his voice barely able to contain his excitement. He began searching the ground for more clues and soon found other pieces of shot and metal armor cast aside. "We must be in the vicinity of the original colony, Master Harris."

"It would seem so. But I'm afraid it will hold few clues. Many have come here but found nothing to tell them what happened to the colony." John took a seat on a fallen log and fumbled for his leather water bag. " 'Twas said the colonists had time to gather most of their belongings. One could say they didn't leave because of an attack but more out of a decision to abandon this place." He gazed at the land. "Maybe they had run out of food. Or winter was coming and they didn't want to be trapped here on some remote piece of land surrounded by water. They had time to gather their possessions and only left behind what they could not carry, like these metal objects."

"Where is Croatoan?" Mark asked. "I heard they had carved such a word on a tree before they left."

John pointed beyond the woods. "West from here, on the mainland. But little remains of the Indian villages there. Most of the Indians moved on to other places."

Mark sighed. "How I wonder where they went. If we knew, then maybe we would have some knowledge of the colonists' whereabouts."

"I think it would do us well to stay here for a little time," Judith said. "Maybe we'll find more clues, if the Indian porters could construct a shelter for us?"

"I will do that," John said hastily. In no time he began wielding an ax, cutting down pine boughs to construct a shelter. Beth watched silently as he took up the thick boughs and tied them together with the rope he had brought. He had seen to their safety, just as he said he would. He had led them here without difficulty. He was even constructing a shelter for them. And soon they would return to Jamestown, perhaps even to embrace a future that was shining brighter to Beth as the journey progressed.

"So when will we see the laughing gulls?" Beth asked him. "And the shells that talk?"

He looked over at her, wiping at his damp face that showed the beginnings of a bemused expression. "Perhaps we can take our leave for a bit with a canoe, and I can show you. 'Tis not far to cross over to another island there in the distance." He acknowledged the strip of land across the water. "There you will see everything I've described to you."

Beth hurried to inquire of Mark if she and John might take the canoe to the land and see the ocean, the seabirds, and the shells. Mark looked between her and John, his face puzzled. "I don't wish you to go unescorted, Beth. Surely we'll all venture there on the morrow."

"But 'tis only to the land there. You can see it from here. We won't be gone long."

"And it might be best to first scout the lay of the land, my lord," John added.

Looking back at Judith, who was busy arranging the shelter for the evening, he finally nodded. "I intend that you be only a scout," he said to John, "and to ensure my sister-in-law's safety and virtue in this venture."

"I give you my word as a Christian gentleman."

He nodded. "Very well."

Beth could hardly wait to begin the venture in the canoe. John picked up the paddle. "What else might we see there?" she inquired breathlessly, barely able to contain her excitement.

"Just remember what I told you," he said.

She closed her eyes to envision it. The endless stretch of sandy coast. Soaring birds like messengers sent from heaven. The talking shells that shared their secrets of the deep. When she opened her eyes, they had traveled quickly toward the new land. "We're like explorers, aren't we?" she said with a sigh. "Going to a land we have never seen. Or rather, one I have never seen."

He laughed. "Beth, you're becoming an explorer, sure and true. Though many would say exploration is not in keeping with a properly reared English lady."

"Many fine ladies did make the journey to Virginia and beyond," she said. "Perhaps I have a bit of my grandparents in me, after all." She didn't realize until then how much Briarwood had kept her imprisoned from life and unable to embrace all the world had to offer. When she stepped onto the land, alone in a vast area of reeds and sand, without a house or living soul to be found, she felt what her grandparents must have felt—a great awe.

"I claim this land for our Savior Christ," Beth said in glee. "Just as the minister of the gospel once did long ago at the founding of Jamestown." Suddenly she heard loud squawking and saw a flock of birds swoop down from above. They seemed to laugh in a way, as if they found her words humorous. "Do the birds mock us?"

"As the lone inhabitants, they only ask why we've come to their home." He looked with satisfaction before pointing southward. "Come. There's more to see."

Along the sandy ground they walked until she could hear a strange sound like a mingled roar that slowly grew as they approached. White breakers formed across the wind-driven water as far as the eye could see. It was the great ocean, the same ocean she had crossed not a few weeks ago. To the left and the right, she saw long stretches of sandy beach with gulls and other seabirds flying in midair.

"What a beautiful sight," she said with a sigh. "When I came here by ship, I only wanted to feel dry land. But now that I can see the ocean without fear, 'tis a grand sight, indeed. No wonder you like it so."

John nodded, sharing the view with her. "It draws me back time and time again. I think often of this place, like a dream that stays with me. My friend Samuel thinks 'tis a part of me and that I should settle here."

"But no one lives here!" she exclaimed. "No one at all. How can you think to settle here all alone?"

"How did other great civilizations come into being? Someone must place his feet on the ground, drive a stake into the land, and call it his own. Then he must take up timbers and build a home." He sighed. "But one person can't survive alone. Civilization can't be built unless there are heirs to possess it for the future. The Roanoke Colony came into being with the idea of establishing a settlement through families." He turned to look at her.

Beth shuffled her feet at the implication. Surely they could not be called a family. Judith and Mark were, yes. Maybe he was thinking that Mark and Judith should be the ones to establish a new settlement. He couldn't be thinking of them together as one, could he? This was not the time or place to consider such things, especially while she was engaged in this new land, the journey, and hoping to discover more about the man who led her here. Maybe one day, if God be willing.

Suddenly he stepped toward her. The wind whipped his hair about him. Again the sleeves of his shirt billowed. He looked perfectly handsome.

"Where are the shells that speak?" Beth inquired hastily, breaking free from the tender look he gave.

John stepped back and searched the surface of the sandy beach. For a time they said nothing, only picked up shells. Beth marveled at the different colors and shapes. She tried to keep her thoughts on her discoveries and not on the way he looked at her just a moment ago as though he might kiss her. What would Mark and Judith say if such a thing occurred?

"I found a small one," John said, coming up behind her. She took the strange shell that looked like a little horn.

"Hold it up to your ear."

She did so and to her delight heard a dull roar, the same sound she'd heard when they first arrived at this place. "Why, it does sound just like the ocean! John, it's true." She was so excited over the discovery, she didn't see him step toward her again until his arms curled around her.

"John. . . ?" she whispered.

He bent his face to greet hers. His eyes softened. His lips found hers. To her surprise, she found herself responding to his kiss. She might have stayed in his embrace, enjoying his warmth and the feel of his lips on hers; but her senses were awakened to what had happened. She stepped out of his embrace. "Please take me back to my sister and brother-in-law. We have been here too long."

"There is no need to be angry, Beth."

She cradled the shell, refusing to meet his gaze. "Take me back. Please."

He said no more but helped her into the canoe. She didn't want to upset him but felt upset herself for having responded to the kiss the way she did. What would Mark and Judith think? If only she had not come to the island. . .but the lure of seeing the ocean and the sand proved too enticing. So, too, did the figure of John in his billowing shirt, with his look of affection that spoke to her heart unlike anything else.

The return journey was begun in silence. They stared at the scenery, all the while pondering what had passed between them. Every so often Beth could sense John searching her face for a reaction. At times, he would heave as if in distress. Finally he rested the paddle inside the canoe. Beth watched in alarm as it slowed to a drift upon the open waters. "W—what are you doing?" She tried to steady her voice. "I asked to be taken back."

"Not until we talk about what happened. I can see you're troubled, but I don't understand why."

Beth raised her head and crossed her arms before her. "My brother-in-law begged you to act as a gentleman and a guide, Mr. Harris. You gave him your word."

"I did act as a gentleman and a guide. But can I help it if I feel led to guide in matters of the heart as well?" He leaned closer. "And you can't pretend to be innocent in this. You enjoyed the kiss as much as I did. Can you deny it?"

Heat quickly entered her cheeks. "How dare you say such things!"

He rested against the bow of the canoe, his gaze unwavering. "Then why did you kiss me back? Surely you sense it, too, that we were meant for each other. The moment we saw each other, we were destined to be together."

"I don't know what you're talking about. But I ask that you return me at once to Roanoke Island. I'm certain my brother-in-law is worried. And I—I pray he doesn't make matters worse for you when he discovers how you betrayed his trust."

John continued to stare at her but with a bemused expression on his face. "Not that I have done any such a thing, but how will he know, pray tell?"

"If I'm asked, I won't deny it."

"There would be no reason for him to ask unless you wish to reveal it. Do what you feel you must when we return. I have done nothing wrong, and neither have you. In fact, it might be better that he knows where we both stand concerning each other." He picked up the paddle.

Beth gnawed on her bottom lip, feeling utter confusion. She did find herself very much attracted to this man, more so than she could have ever hoped or dreamed. How she'd longed for a man to notice her and to fall in love with her. But was that man supposed to be John Harris? The guide of their trip? The one with a strange past, who could vacillate from love and concern to anger and vengeance? And the one who even now looked at her with such tenderness, she could scarcely draw a breath?

The trip concluded in silence. Returning to the camp, Beth saw that Judith already had a cooking fire ablaze. The Indian porters had arrived with fish, lanced by the long spears they had made. "Did you see the ocean, Beth?" Judith asked.

Beth could feel John's presence behind her as if daring her to tell her sister what had transpired between them. "Yes. It—'twas lovely. We saw the laughing gulls." She hesitated. "And we. . .we. . ."

"What? Tell me everything."

"We. . .we found a shell that sounds just like the ocean."

Again she sensed it—John's silence that spoke louder than any words. *Are you going to tell them that I'm a betrayer of their trust? Or that you also shared in the kiss?* She choked down the words that began to rise in her throat even as Mark arrived.

"I'm glad you returned safely," he said with a smile.

"Perhaps soon you can take me there, Master Harris. I'm very curious to see all of this Hatorask for myself."

"As you wish, my lord."

Judith and Mark both returned to the dinner at hand, even as Beth went to the water barrel to refresh herself.

"I knew you wouldn't say anything," John whispered huskily, his face lightening, even as he scooped up water to splash on his face.

She whirled. "Maybe not now, but I may need to. . . ."

He only smiled. "Even so, we are meant to be together. You know it as well as I. And to betray this would mean betraying yourself." He shook his hands dry and left in a flourish.

Beth returned to the water in the barrel, which rippled with her dusky and distressed image reflected on the glassy surface. *Dear Lord, what am I to believe? If this is all good and true, please show me before I forsake my heart for something that isn't meant to be!*

eight

John set about gathering more wood for the evening fire, though his thoughts were a jumble. He knew the encounter had startled Beth and perhaps even himself, but he couldn't help how he felt. And he was certain she felt the same way. Whether she denied it or not, she had responded to his kiss with equal fervor. Why she insisted, then, on toying with his emotions—even going so far as to threaten discussing the encounter with her brother-in-law—went beyond his sense of reasoning. He had expected demureness but instead found a woman of independence and strong will. Perhaps it came from the harsh life she'd endured in England, caring for her ailing father and running a large estate. He wasn't certain whether he would be able to bear up under such things, but he asked God for grace. Beth meant too much to him to let her go. And in time, with gentleness, she would embrace a sound future with him as her husband.

Besides, it might do us well if she acted upon her threat and told her brother-in-law about us, he mused, nearly chuckling aloud, even as he continued to gather wood for the evening fire. *Maybe the whole world should know, from the land to the sea. But now is not the right time, not with Beth feeling so uncertain.* Since the encounter at the sandy beach, she stayed a good distance away from him, though he could see her glancing in his direction every so often. When she did, a flush would tint her cheeks a delicate red. The reaction told him she must still be interested, that God was at work, and in due time their relationship would strengthen. In the meantime he would be patient.

John unloaded wood by the blazing fire, pushing it into a pile. Then he asked Mark if he required anything else of him.

"Yes, as a matter of fact, there is." Mark motioned for him to follow him to a place within the wooded glade, away from the camp. "Judith couldn't help but notice that something seems to be troubling Beth. Do you know what it could be?"

John found himself speechless at first. *Dare I tell him right now that we have fallen in love and we declared our love with a kiss?* He was uncertain how such news would be received. After all, this man had entrusted his sister-in-law to him and asked him to safeguard her virtue. He might face condemnation or worse. He decided to stay silent until he knew Beth's heart and matters were as clear between them as fresh water. "I'm certain the journey has been quite overwhelming for her," he finally said.

"She doesn't appear to be herself. I only wonder if perhaps something passed between you both on your journey to the other island."

Now it was John's turn to feel the warmth of a flush enter his cheeks. Mark knew everything. Beth must have acted on her threat and told him. And now he needed to heal the breach and swiftly.

He opened his mouth to speak when Mark said, "Did you have some manner of disagreement between yourselves, perhaps?"

John sighed so loudly that Mark raised an eyebrow. *No, she didn't tell him about our kiss.* "More a wonder, my lord, with all the coast has to offer," he said in haste. "The sand. The gulls and the shells. Other things. Perhaps it was too much for her."

Mark nodded. "Yes, she did tell us about the glorious things she had seen. Perhaps it's mere sorrow that she can't remain there. I must say, I find the description intriguing. I would like you to take me there early on the morrow so I can see this place for myself."

"Certainly. I would be honored. 'Tis a grand place, unspoiled and rich." *A place where love can take root and find a place to dwell*, he thought.

"We will all go there at sunup," he declared. "You and Beth can then show us what you have seen."

John nodded and returned to the fire where Beth was busy cooking. They came so close to each other, the sleeves of their garments brushed. Beth jerked back as though he had touched her with a thorny branch.

"Did you tell him?" she whispered fiercely. "I saw you both talking."

"We talked about many things."

She withdrew, her eyes large, her mouth falling open in astonishment. "How could you do such a thing? I'm now disgraced in his eyes."

"Calm yourself, madam. I only told him about the journey to the beach and the wonder of it. And he wants to see it. But pray tell, to what are you referring?"

"You know very well what I speak of. Why do you make light of it?"

"Believe me, I take this quite seriously. If you don't see it already, I'm in love with you. And I believe it might be mutual."

She gasped and returned to the cooking, even as Judith came forward, her face all smiles. "I heard the plan!" Judith called out. "So we will go see the ocean and all these wonders you speak of, Mr. Harris. How grand, indeed."

"Very grand," he agreed with a sideways glance to Beth, whose cheeks grew even rosier than the fairest rose in an English garden. When Judith disappeared, he turned back to see the water in the jug rippling in Beth's shaking hands.

"How can you do this to me?" Beth murmured, heaving the jug to the ground, even as water splashed a mottled print on her dress. "You know nothing of what I feel."

"If I'm so wrong, then you have nothing to fear. But you know I'm not. I loved you the moment you stepped onto this land. This place has grown much more inviting by your charm."

"You speak senseless words."

"If they are senseless words, then I'm made senseless by your presence." He saw it then, a flicker of appreciation in her face, her eyes softening, her lips upturned—dare he think—into the semblance of a smile? Then a thought passed through her, and the frown returned.

"You mustn't say anything about what happened between us in that place when we return to the sands."

"I have no plans to do so, madam. But didn't you once threaten to tell everything anyway?" He couldn't help but smile, even as he could see her discomfort rise with each passing moment. "I guess there is no longer such a threat."

"I only said what I shall do should the need arise. Just be careful. Please."

John had never felt more hope than he did at that moment. *I know our destinies are linked, even as you sense it now, my dear Beth. Even if you can't speak of it, the time will come when you can. And when it is time, you will be my wife and we will make our home together by the ocean.*

❧

With Beth in his presence, John found it difficult to stay his thoughts on his duties as keeper of their canoe and guide to the far reaches. He rowed swiftly, noting the excitement on the faces of both Mark and Judith in the other canoe and then the trepidation that sent tense lines running across Beth's forehead. Despite the hat she wore, deep tones, painted by the wind and sun, replaced the paleness that once washed her cheeks. At times she complained to her sister about her complexion. He thought her fairer than any woman he had seen. Even now, he wanted to gaze longingly at her fine features, but she had turned aside. The large straw hat blocked his view of her. She kept one hand on her hat to keep the wind from stealing it away.

He made haste for the island, thinking how much this place had awakened his senses when he first arrived here several years ago and did so again when he brought Beth to its shores. The first time he came here it had been a simple exploratory trip to see all there was to see. He could still remember Robert's exclamations as he ran along the beach and then fell face first into a sandy bank, laughing all the while.

"I want to build my home here, John," Robert had told him.

"And a perfect place it would be, too," he had replied.

"There is not a soul to be found anywhere."

John glanced up, half expecting his brother to have uttered the comment. Instead he heard Mark shout and point out the vacant area devoid of people. Only the plants and animals lived there, placed by the hand of the Creator. John easily brought the canoe to rest at an embankment. Mark helped Judith out of their boat. Together they headed across the island toward the roar of the distant ocean. John waited as Beth slowly gathered herself, appearing as if she didn't want to leave the security of the canoe.

"You have nothing to fear, madam," he whispered to her. "Our secret is safe."

"I fear nothing," she retorted. But clearly she looked troubled at returning to the place where their love for each other had been kindled in a kiss. Why would she feel such discontent and not pure joy? Unless she truly didn't experience the same love he felt for her. He frowned, wishing he could read her thoughts. But they remained as private as the confines of her heart and indiscernible to his curious eye. Beth was leaving him more and more puzzled as time went by.

He followed her as she made her way to the beach where Mark and Judith stood looking at the ocean. "What a magnificent place," Mark acknowledged, "as if Almighty God had just spoken the word and formed it all. An unspoiled and rich land, indeed." He made haste down the shore, with the others struggling to keep up.

"I've often thought of settling here," John admitted. "Jamestown and the area around the river James are growing thick with colonists. But this land of Carolana has few to call its own. An unspoiled land, as you say, just waiting to be inhabited."

"I can see why such a place would be tempting," Judith added. "Don't you agree, Beth?"

John waited for her answer, only to see her nod. She was staring at the ocean. "Are you thinking of England?" he asked.

"I'm thinking of the people and places that do exist far away from here," Beth admitted. "The homes and the lands. If one were to set sail on a boat, they would come to such a land in due time. It seems hard to believe."

"Are you wishing you were there still?"

She turned then, the hat she wore casting a shadow across

her face. "Now why would you think that, Mr. Harris?" She wandered off to join her sister.

John didn't know why. Maybe searching for evidence in her heart, just as the sisters now began searching the sand for shells.

Just then, John heard a shout of exclamation from Mark. He turned, his hand instinctively touching his pistol at his waist. Judith ran up to Mark, gripping his arm as he pointed in the far-off distance. John squinted to see several figures approaching, walking swiftly along the sandy shore. At first he thought they might be fellow explorers. As they drew closer, he could plainly see the shocks of dark hair flowing in the breeze, and the tawny-colored complexion inherent to the Indians of the land. His muscles tensed at the sight. His fingers closed around the snaphaunce pistol, slowly drawing it.

"Calm yourself, Mr. Harris," Mark said to him. "They have shown no aggression. Let's find out what they want."

John wanted to answer to the contrary but kept his emotions at bay. At the same time, Beth drew closer to him as if seeking his protection. "What could they want?" she asked, her voice fearful.

"Just stay by me."

"Welcome," a voice announced.

They all stared at each other in amazement at the greeting uttered in English. Upon closer inspection, John could see that these Indians were not of the sort he had seen at Jamestown. Their eyes lacked the fierce color like the black of night concealing some mischief. Maybe it was the sun reflecting in them. Even their skin lacked the deep earthy tones of the Indians in Jamestown.

"Thank you," Mark answered. "We are from a great

white man's village up north called Jamestown. I am Mark Reynolds. This is my wife, Judith, my sister-in-law, Elizabeth, and our guide, John Harris."

"Welcome," the Indian repeated. "We good friends."

A strange statement to make, John thought. *How can we be friends when we have only just been introduced?* He fought to bury his misgivings even as they surfaced quicker than he could drive them back. He looked each of them over carefully while his fingers caressed the hilt of his pistol. *If they but flinch in the wrong direction, they will wish they hadn't.*

"How is it we're friends?" Mark asked.

"We good friends of the white man. He come much and we bring him to village." The Indian pointed down the coastline, far into the distance.

"You mean that other white men have come before us?" Mark asked. John detected the excitement escalating in the man's voice. Surely Mark couldn't mean that these Indians knew the colonists from long ago?

"Some stay. Some go."

"They must be from the village called Sandbanks," John said to Mark in a low, even voice.

"Are there white men now in your village of Sandbanks?" Mark asked the Indian.

"Some stay, some go," he repeated. "You welcome in village."

Mark turned, his eyes wide, his lips upturned into a smile. "Glory be! The Indian talks of white men visiting their village. Maybe they came long ago, such as those from the Roanoke Colony. This could be our answer, sent from heaven above."

"That can't be, my lord," John interjected. "It has been sixty years. Surely they speak of other explorers who have come here." Even as he said it, he knew Mark didn't believe him. He chose instead to cling to his stubborn faith without any evidence that his wife's relatives or the colony had found refuge with the Indians. *Refuge indeed with such people. As if that were ever possible!*

"We must find out," Mark announced. "We will go with them to their village."

John stared, unable to believe what he'd heard. "But you can't mean it. You know nothing about them or in what manner they speak. How can you blindly stumble into their village, not knowing what lies there?"

"Faith, Master Harris. A belief that God has guided our footsteps. He allowed you to guide us to the Roanoke Island and then to this place where we were fortunate enough to meet the Indians. We have no cause to think they wish us harm. And if they do know of other English colonists from long ago, then it is only right that we seek them out and inquire."

John looked to Beth for her opinion. She only stood passively by, watching the scene unfold before her. Perhaps he could at least convince Mark to allow him to safeguard the women, to take them back to Roanoke Island while Mark went seeking the information he wished. When he broached it, Judith shook her head, clinging to her husband's arm. "Where he goes, I go, too. 'Tis my relatives we seek, after all."

"Surely you are not going also," John asked Beth in a low voice.

"Why shouldn't I? I trust my sister's husband. He won't lead us astray. And I think there may be something important there for us to discover."

He fought to come up with a reasonable excuse. How he

wished he could tell her that if anything happened to her, he would cease to live. That he could not trust the one he loved to a people he knew nothing about. "Don't do this. Let us return to Roanoke."

"Alone and unescorted? Really, Mr. Harris."

"I'm thinking of you, madam, whom I pledged to safeguard when I undertook this journey."

"Can you not let go of your suspicions of the naturals for a moment?"

"Suspicion is also a manner of wisdom. A moment is all it takes for something to go wrong. And it's unwise to stumble into an Indian village just because one of them speaks English. It could be a clever trap."

"Then you must come along and be our guard," she said with a teasing lilt to her voice.

He sighed. *They don't know nor do they understand. They follow blindly after their own ambitions without giving a thought as to what might lay hidden.*

John hated feeling this way. He hated not knowing the tactics of this adversary in the Carolana region. If these Indians were like the others, they had weapons of cunning and evil. The ability to draw out a helpless prey and then pounce when one least expected it. He glanced over at Beth, even as the ocean breeze took up her brown hair. The straw hat she had worn to protect her from the sun had fallen behind her neck, allowing her hair to dance upon the wind. How could he let her walk into that place and put her life in peril? If only she would listen.

❧

For a long time they walked until the journey took them away from the sandy shores and into the woods. Mark engaged in conversation as much as he could with the

Indians, inquiring again of the white men who had come and gone. The Indians only smiled and shook their heads. Either they could not answer him or they refused to answer.

"Be patient," Judith admonished her husband. "We'll soon discover all there is to know."

"But I'm hopeful," he admitted. "To think that God has guided our very footsteps. And we have no one to thank but Master Harris. If he hadn't led us to these shores, we would never have met them."

"Yes, thank you, Mr. Harris," Judith echoed.

John could hardly accept such appreciation with the ill will brewing inside him. Reluctantly following the Indians along a well-worn path and then to a bank by the sound waters where they boarded canoes, he grew more agitated. If only he could convince them all to turn back, to retreat to Roanoke Island before it was too late. At least for Beth's sake. Maybe, just maybe, he could attempt one last time to convince her.

He came alongside her, opening his mouth, ready to speak the words on his heart. Instead Beth purred, "Just think, another adventure about to happen. 'Tis good you are going, Mr. Harris, for adventure is a part of you. And I must admit, I'm quite eager to know if they have had any contact with other English."

"Even if I tell you a secret about these people that may cause you to reconsider?"

She glanced back. "What secret?"

"You may not wish to meet them once I tell you."

She frowned. "You're going to tell me they are violent. And they have shown nothing of violence."

"I only say it might do well to hide your eyes when we arrive," he told her.

"From what, pray tell?"

"The savages, that is, the Indians of this place are not known to keep proper dress. They wear little clothing. You will find it quite immoral to your eyes."

She frowned. "Mr. Harris, how can you say such things? You only want me to turn aside, to return with you instead to Roanoke."

"I speak the truth, to prepare you, if you would only listen."

Her cheeks warmed. "I refuse to concern myself with such things. I know this land and the people are very different from England. I've seen it already." She settled herself quickly into a canoe.

"But do you understand just how different? And not just the animals like the aroughcun I spoke about with its black eyes or the seabirds with their large beaks. There are also people here you have never seen, who do things you wouldn't think civilized people could do. Who act and dress in a way you may have never imagined."

She hesitated. In that moment, John saw a spark of hope. Then she raised her head and leveled her gaze at him. "I will look on them as God does, as His creation made in His image. It will help, don't you think?"

"Perhaps for a time," he managed to say before retreating to help paddle a canoe. There was little doubt that Beth's faith paralleled her brother-in-law's, with their determination equal. John once thought he had such faith, too. He had trusted God many times for the circumstances of his life. Sometimes it took faith just to rise and face a new dawn, especially in this land. Faith to keep going when everything looked bleak. But Mark had turned the idea of faith into some reckless need for knowledge, set with unrealistic goals that would only be met by sadness. Yet what could John do? There was nothing left to do. Beth's brown eyes glimmered with anticipation, her lips parted, appearing as eager as her sister and brother-in-law to see this village of Sandbanks and find out about the English that had come and gone. Much to his chagrin, they were all one in their quest. If they were insistent on following the Indians, he must go as well. But his hand would not be far from his pistol. He would be ready. For all they knew, it could turn out to be their saving grace.

nine

After many hours of travel by land and by water, the village of Sandbanks appeared before them. Crescent-shaped wooden homes, covered with bark, stood in a semicircle. Cooking fires burned before each of the homes, laying a thick blanket of smoke over the area. Indians began to emerge from dwellings or from the nearby brush where they tended to the duties of the day, as if the arrival of the party had sent out an alarm among them. Beth pointed at the little children who hovered near their mothers. John wondered if she would also acknowledge the lack of dress, especially among the women. But she gave no such sign of alarm, or if she felt any, kept it well hidden. In fact, her peace with the situation that would horrify any lady of England continued to amaze him.

"Welcome," exclaimed a rather tall Indian, no doubt one of the leaders of the village. "Where come you?"

"Virginia," Mark said. "We seek family of ours who were lost long ago."

The leader looked to several of his councilors. They muttered amongst themselves. "Who lost?" the leader asked.

"They came from a ship many years ago," Mark tried to explain. "On a ship that went through the Great Waters from their homeland far away. There were men, women, and children on board that ship."

The leader shook his head.

John wanted desperately to tell Mark that these Indians knew nothing, that the Roanoke Colony had long since vanished, the people's whereabouts known to God alone. Their quest for knowledge had been of no avail in his opinion, until he heard Beth encouraging Mark to continue his inquiry and not give up hope. He held back any attempt to intervene. There was Beth to consider, after all. These were her relatives they sought. She was emotionally bound to the quest. And, in turn, he must keep alive his own personal quest to make Beth his, no matter what else transpired on this journey.

They were led into one of the larger dwellings in the village, where the leaders fed them food as they sat upon woven mats. John stayed alert to everything around him, knowing he might be depended upon if trouble arose. Mark continued to parley with them through words and signs as if they were his friends. Even Beth and Judith appeared interested in everything the Indians had to say—speaking of the lands around them and the possibility of encountering Englishmen from past ships. But try as he might to stay confident, John couldn't help envisioning some terrible scene—an ambush while they reclined in the council house, the Indians doing away with them, one by one, as they slept, or scheming some other fiendish plot.

"Wise One know things," the leader of the village finally admitted to Mark. "Wise One know English long ago."

Mark sat up on his knees, barely able to contain his excitement. "May I speak with this wise one? It is very important."

"He go to Great Spirit. Return when sun down."

John wondered if Mark could wait that long. John had eaten a bit of the fish given to them, but found his appetite sated. If only they could find out what they needed to know and be done with this village and the people.

When time had passed and John saw little sign of danger in their midst, he left the council house, hoping to find peace by the shores of the sound. The sun had begun to dip low, reflecting its orange tint upon the waters. He pondered the wisdom of ever having accepted this task of guiding the family to Hatorask. Though he loved the land, and yes, the woman who accompanied them on the journey, he wondered if it had been a wise decision. Someone like his friend Samuel, who also knew the lay of the land, could have easily led them here. But likely, if John had stayed in Jamestown, so, too, would the pain from the past. Nothing would have been reconciled, as Samuel wisely warned. He faced it when he first saw the Indian couriers, and now he relived it every moment he remained in this village. It was like some unseen spirit forcing him headlong into a battle for his soul. "But I don't want to confront this," he voiced aloud. "Not here. Not now. Not ever. Can't I be at peace?"

"John, what troubles you?"

He spun about as if an angel had sung the question from the heavens above. He had not even heard the faint footsteps of Beth, who had come up behind him. Had she witnessed everything, even the groaning of his heart?

"I—I only pray we might leave here soon," he said hastily. "We still have our camp at Roanoke Island and our possessions there, you know."

Beth shook her head. "I hardly think that is what ails you. You said something about being at peace."

His cheeks flamed. " 'Tis nothing."

"But something surely troubles you. What is it?"

Why does she ask me these things? Can't she see I have no will to speak about this? That I refuse to do so?

"Do you still think the Indians will harm us?"

"No. They seem of a different sort than those who live near Jamestown."

Beth stood beside him, sharing in the sunset that graced the landscape. "Then what? I only wish you would share your troubling thoughts with me."

"Beth, you have secrets in your heart, I'm sure. Things known only to God so that God, alone, can bear them. Maybe even deep things concerning your father, for instance, that no one else could ever understand. Will you trust that I, too, have things I believe only God can carry? That no one, especially someone like you, need be concerned by them?"

Beth stood still and silent as if considering it. "Yes, I do know that we all carry deep secrets within. But I know, too, that one day they need to be reconciled, lest they dig away at us and leave us in a grave." She turned to him. "And I truly believe those secrets have allowed your peace to escape, and you are in some dark grave. It may be why you're so angry."

"When I'm with you, I have more peace than I could ever want." He reached for her hand, but she kept it tucked away.

She chuckled uncomfortably. "You're quite mistaken if you think I'm of a peaceful sort. I've contended with more trouble that only God could know. And I've had my trials. But I also know I needed to confide in those closest to me. To allow others to help bear my burdens. Find someone to help bear your burden, John. And let it go."

Just then they heard Mark calling for them to come attend the meeting. The Indian called Wise One had returned from his time of meditation.

"Will you come?" she asked.

"Of course." If anything, he did wish to know if there existed some answer to the mystery of the long-lost colony. But he could not forget the words that echoed in his thoughts.

"Find someone to help bear your burden, John. And let it go."

❧

The name *Wise One* fit well the elder Indian seated before them. But there were other striking features about him. A face nearly white in color, if wrinkled with age. Hair a dark brown with eyes to match. If John were not mistaken, the Indian could have surely been a white man at one time, even sitting there clothed in apparel bedecked in beads and accoutrements of the village. When he began speaking, John's curiosity rose further. Mark and the women stirred, too, as if they had come to a similar conclusion.

"There are pictures of ships," Wise One said, "painted on lodgings long ago. Say ships from the Great Waters with white men. One call white men friends. Spoke kindly to them. Helped them when their leader went to Great Waters."

"The women here. . .it is their grandparents who were a part of that ship," Mark explained. "But they were lost like the rest. No one knows what happened."

"They say many left. Some here. Some far away."

Judith grabbed Beth's hand. "Some did come here! Oh Beth, did you hear what he said?"

"What of the name Colman?" Mark pressed. "Does that name sound familiar to you?

"A cold man?"

"No. Colman. Thomas and Susanna Colman. Have you ever heard of them?"

Wise One shook his head. "No cold man here. I speak stories told me. We all there is."

"But you look as if you may have English blood in you."

The Indian stared long and hard. John stirred in discomfort at the frown that suddenly erupted on the Indian's wizened face. He wondered what it meant. Perhaps the Indian knew of something in his past, if English blood had mingled with Indian, although Wise One said nothing of this.

"I Wise One of the Croatoan people."

"I'm sorry. I didn't mean to offend you. I only wanted to know if the English did live among you."

Wise One stood. "It is as I say." With that he left.

The air grew still and silent. John wondered once more if all this had been in vain. But after a moment of silence, Mark hailed it an achievement of the greatest importance. "Praise be. We know much."

"But our relatives could be anywhere," Judith said with a sigh.

"Perhaps. But we know now that many from the colony did survive. They were not massacred or left to die of disease. That some found refuge among the Indians. And for all you know, some of these Indians could be related to the white men."

Judith stared at him, aghast. "That can't be! My relatives are not Indians!"

"Not yours, but there may be others from the colony. You see with your eyes how Wise One appears. He must have English blood somewhere in his lineage, even if he denies it. Many do in this village. Even if some have left, there are others here that bear the characteristics."

"If only one of them knew the name of Colman," she mourned.

"But Wise One did hear of the English. Those that came in ships. The stories that have been passed down. So be of good cheer. Our journey has not been in vain." Mark paused, then added, "We'll stay a few days longer, learning all we can. And maybe Wise One will remember other things that could be of great importance to us."

Inwardly, John groaned. He didn't find this news cheerful in the least. A few more days in this village to him would feel like months—and more time for further contemplation while existing among those who kindled memories of a pain-filled past.

Despite Mark's wish to remain and the way the rest of the family knit themselves with the Indian village, John did his best to separate himself from it all. One of them needed to keep sense in all this. John put it upon himself to remain on alert, though it pained him to see the family move easily among the Indians. Mark went out with several of the villagers to try his hand at spearfishing. Beth decided to do some beadwork using the gut of animals as the thread, enjoying the older Indian woman who taught her the skill. She laughed in glee as several children came up to her, tapping her on the back, then jumping away as she tried to catch them. *Soften your heart, John,* he admonished himself. *These Indians have shown no aggression whatsoever. They have only been hospitable and kind.* Yet he could not help sensing his own personal departure from it all as if he were separated by some wide void, unable to communicate or enjoy a different way of life.

When it came time for the evening meal, Mark proudly offered as the main course the fish he had lanced with a homemade spear. "I rather fancied it," he said with a grin. Everyone helped themselves to large portions of fish cooked over hot stones. No one seemed to notice that John, again, ate little.

"And I see you made yourself a necklace," Mark observed, nodding toward Beth.

She wore an innocent grin. "Isn't it lovely? I like this place very much. And I even had one of the women tell me about her belief in the Creator God. These people seem to have a bit of understanding of the Christian God. Someone must have told them."

"Surely it wasn't an explorer," Mark mused. His gaze locked with John's. "That is not to say an explorer cannot be a believer. But from what I've heard about them, they are more intent on finding treasure than spreading the gospel."

"I suppose treasure is in the eye of the beholder," John said. "Treasures don't have to come by way of possession but sometimes in some idle quest, as well."

Mark put down his corn bread. "I see. Surely you don't believe we are still on some 'idle quest,' as you put it. Our quest is being fulfilled by God."

"And how is that, my lord? You know little more than when you first arrived. You see an Indian that might bear resemblance to the English, who knows a few tales passed down from the ages, and you believe this is your answer?" John saw the looks radiating in his direction.

"I believe more hope has been found here than any witnessed since the colony disappeared. And I think when we return to Jamestown, we should send news of our discovery and bring hope to those who, like us, lost loved ones."

"But the colonists remain lost. You have found no trace of them still."

Mark said no more, but John could see his opinion had dampened the companionship of the meal and the joy from the meeting with Wise One.

Again he took time that evening to contemplate. There would be no Beth by his side this night as he gazed out over the waters. She had looked at him in dismay during the meal, as if his words had quenched the flame of hope within them all. Despite what they thought, he sought the truth. To him, enough was enough. His mission here had been completed. He had fulfilled his duties as guide and protector. They had seen to their quest, as futile as it had been. Now the time was drawing nigh for his personal quest to come forth. He would see it happen and then remove himself from this village and from the past as quickly as possible.

ten

Beth uttered a sigh of despair as she walked among the reeds, thinking of the last few days. If only there were a way to break through. If only she knew the secret to reaching a hard heart. Kindness had always seemed to work with her father, whose heart was as hard as any stone fit for a wall. Kindness and a merciful heart. Drawing near with an ear ready to listen. But none of those things seemed to break the hard heart of John Harris. He remained aloof, trapped in some foreign land of his own making. She had thought with the attraction between them that something would reach inside him, that the pain he kept buried would be brought forth.

She considered her own actions of late. Maybe if she hadn't reacted the way she did after the kiss they shared—playing with the emotion of it all, threatening to inform Mark of their encounter when she knew she would never do such a thing. John had seemed amused by the antics, but now she realized it had been wrong. She should be open with her feelings if she expected him to be open with his. She should have told him that she did enjoy his kiss and his companionship, that she was inquiring of God if they were meant to be together or if this was for a season and God had other plans for them to embrace. She contemplated sharing these thoughts, in the hope that he would respond favorably, but was uncertain how to go about it.

Instead, she returned to the village and immersed herself

in making a string of beads. Soon a young Indian girl with a broken front tooth joined her and, at once, took it upon herself to show Beth how to string the beads in vivid color combinations. The girl did not speak English very well, so communication was a challenge. But between the hand symbols and single words, they were able to tell each other their names and share a little about their families. The young girl's name was translated to Rising Star, which Beth liked very much. Beth then pointed to Judith, who stood in the distance.

"My sister," she told Rising Star.

The girl called forth a chubby little Indian boy and said, "Sister." Beth nearly laughed until she realized Rising Star thought *sister* meant sibling. "You mean brother."

"Brother," the girl repeated and laughed.

Just then, Beth caught sight of John staring at her. At first he seemed irritated that she sat with Rising Star, making Indian beadwork. Then he offered the semblance of a crooked smile, which set her mind at ease. He shifted a sack of supplies over one shoulder as if he were ready to go somewhere. "Are you going fishing with the men this morning, Mr. Harris?" Beth called out.

"I'm going back to Roanoke Island to break camp. Your brother-in-law asked me to retrieve your belongings from there."

Beth considered accompanying him but knew Mark would never approve. And after what happened the last time they were together, she wasn't certain she should. But the lure of being with him was strong. And there were things hidden in the dark that needed to be brought to light. She glanced back at the young girl. "Maybe Rising Star and I could go with you, just to the coast. Maybe we could find some of those talking shells. 'Tis a pretty day."

John gaped for a moment then shook his head. "There's no need."

"Why? I think 'tis a fine idea, and I'm sure she would like it. Wait for me."

Beth stood to her feet, determined to seek out Rising Star's mother and see if the girl could accompany her. At least it would give her time to be with John Harris under the guise of going to see the ocean. When Beth communicated to the Indian woman of going with the white man to see the great ocean, the woman hesitated at first. "Rising Star like you, Beth Cold Wo-man. She like Great Waters. Yes, she go."

"Thank you!" Beth hurried to inform Judith that she was taking Rising Star on a journey in John's company.

When she returned, John had already begun heading for the trail that led back to the canoes. The canoes would take them through the sound waters and farther up the coast. At first he said nothing. Finally, when Rising Star was occupied, he turned to Beth. "Why are you really coming? 'Tis a long journey, as you well know."

She saw his gaze focus on Rising Star. "You aren't dismayed she is going. . . ?"

"No, of course not. I thought you would want to stay at the village. You seemed to have found a home there and many new friends."

Beth smiled as Rising Star raced along the path toward the canoes beached by the waters, laughing all the while. "Isn't she sweet? She's like having a younger sister. She sits by my side, helping me make the beaded necklaces. Isn't God good, John?"

John heaved the canoe into the water, then helped them each aboard. "Certainly He is good. Sometimes I don't understand everything He does. I know it must be for good and not for evil, and that all things work together for His purposes. I only wish it were not such a mystery."

Beth sucked in her breath. *Remember, Beth. Show kindness and mercy.* Maybe he would use this time to unfetter the burdens of his heart. Perhaps God had set apart this place and time for new things to emerge out of things that were old and no more. "Sometimes His ways are difficult to understand, I know. I guess that's what faith is all about. To believe and trust even when we don't understand. To accept His will and know He wants what's best for us."

"Surely you found it difficult to accept that after what you went through in England with your father."

" 'Twas difficult," she admitted. "Many nights I cried myself to sleep. But then I would wake up to find the sun shining in my window and see that God had made all things new. A new day, indeed. And I had a father who needed me, even if he was not right in the mind."

John stared at the open waters before them, paddling fiercely. "Did the physicians ever find out what was wrong with him?"

"No. Of course, after all that was shared about Father's losing his parents with the colony and his desire to find them, I wondered if his ill mind came from that loss. 'Tis hard to know what things can cause us to slip away out of despair and questioning. When Judith told me about Father's longing to find his parents, I had no idea he thought that way. It lay buried in him for so long. I pray it didn't drive him mad."

They talked for a long time about their families and their lives in England. When they finally arrived at the part of the island not far from where Beth and John first shared in the kiss, Rising Star leaped out of the canoe and raced along to the great ocean. It wasn't long before she found a shell, the same kind Beth had used to listen to the ocean sounds. She helped the young girl hold it to her ear and then pointed to the ocean before them. "A talking shell," she explained. Beth again felt familiar warmth at those words. She recalled how her own encounter with the shell led to the kiss. When she found John looking at her, she could sense that he, too, was reflecting on that time. But now everything was different. Even though the time was but a short bit ago, it seemed like ages past.

"I must leave now for Roanoke Island," John said, gazing at her. "I won't be too far gone. You can see the island from here."

"I'm sure we will find plenty to do while you're away."

He paused, staring at her as if wishing he could give her a kiss good-bye. Again a tingle rose up within her at the mere thought. But, at the last moment, he turned away for the canoe and his own journey to the distant island.

While he was gone, Beth spent the time with Rising Star, helping her with English words to describe the scenery before them. "Creator God made them all," Beth told her. "The sky, the ocean, even you."

"Great Spirit?"

"The Creator God is a Great Spirit, but also the one true God. A God of love. And He sent His Son Jesus to die for us so that we can live with Him forever in His home in heaven."

"Me see Jesus," said Rising Star. "Me go to heaven with Beth Cold Man."

Beth wanted to embrace the young girl. How might one show Jesus to her? She gazed at the island in the distance where John had gone. How they did need to show Jesus to these people. How to forgive. How to love. How to be salt and light in everything. But how difficult it could be as well, not only to speak of her faith but to live it, too. She realized it more than ever, with everything that had happened in this journey. A journey that tested not only her body and spirit but her heart as well.

Beth sat down in the sand and began shaping it into mounds. Rising Star laughed at her antics. She pretended to fashion the corn cakes as she had done on so many occasions during the long trip. Watching Rising Star make her own set of sand cakes, she wondered about Josephine, the servant who had helped at Briarwood and who had been like a sister to her. Before they separated, Josephine told her she was going to London to try to find her family. Beth murmured a prayer for her friend, hoping she did have a joyful reunion with her loved ones.

Time passed quickly. Evening shadows began to fall. Beth grew concerned for the late hour and stood to her feet, shaking sand out of her skirts. Rising Star was content to gather a mound of tiny shells with which to make more necklaces when they arrived back at the village. Beth instead looked westward, toward Roanoke Island, wondering what could be keeping John. Visions assaulted her then—from his boat tipping over, spilling him into the waters, to some surprise attack that left him wounded and helpless on the island.

"Look, look, Beth Cold Man," Rising Star said, showing her the many shell fragments she had collected.

"They will make a beautiful necklace." Again Beth gazed toward Roanoke Island. The sun had already begun its journey to the distant horizon. It would be dark before they arrived back.

At last she spotted a small vessel on the shimmering waters and murmured a prayer of relief. "Where have you been?" she demanded when he paddled up.

John raised his eyebrow at her. "There was another exploration party on the island. I met two of the men there—Anderson and Edgar. They talked about their party. Even mentioned having a reverend with them—I suppose for their spiritual guidance."

"Have you ever seen them before?"

John shook his head. "Many are starting to come here, looking for new land in which to settle. And 'tis well I went today to the island, or all your possessions would have become their booty. I had to do some bargaining to get back what I could.

"Oh, no," Beth mourned. "I thought our Indian porters would still be there at the camp."

"There was no sign of them. They likely left when we didn't return. But all is well. I even brought back your cloak." He held it up, winking as he did. "But let us make haste. Come into the boat. We should be back to the village by nightfall if we leave now."

Beth called for Rising Star. Soon they were off with John, paddling southward toward Sandbanks. Beth said little but soon became keenly aware that he was looking at her. Finally she asked, "Is there something you wish?"

"Just my curiosity, madam. Perhaps my eyes were deceiving me, but could it be you were concerned for my welfare back on the shore?"

" 'Twas growing late, Mr. Harris, and we have a young one here that must be returned to the village. I'm certain her mother is very worried."

The paddle assaulted the water with each stroke. "Is that all?"

"I don't understand what you're hinting at."

"Perhaps I only imagined a fair and desperate woman by the shore then, anxious for my return."

"You do think highly of yourself, don't you?"

"Only if I believe a woman cares for me. Then perhaps my life holds value."

Beth shook her head and looked down to find Rising Star observing their exchange with interest. "He your man, Beth Cold Man?" she asked.

Beth couldn't believe what the young girl had said. She choked and began coughing.

"What did she say?" John asked. "I don't know if I heard her right."

"Nothing. Nothing at all."

"I think I heard her ask if I was your man. Providential words, don't you think?"

"Please. . .we mustn't speak of it."

He said no more, much to her relief. In fact, neither of them said anything while they made haste toward the Indian village. Arriving at the shore, they walked through the rushes with only the moon to light their way, until they saw golden flickers and smelled the acrid odor of cooking fires tainting the night air.

Rising Star bubbled over with news of her journey to her Indian family and friends, showing them her collection of shells. Beth recognized Judith, who came into the firelight with concern etched in lines running across her face. "Where have you been, Beth? 'Tis long past sundown!"

"John spent time on Roanoke Island with some other explorers who nearly made off with our possessions. But I'm glad I took Rising Star with me. I was able to share a little of God's holy Word with her. And Judith, she told me she wants to see Jesus."

"I'm glad, Beth. I only wish you didn't forget yourself on these trips you take with Master Harris. I must say, it seems a marriage covenant is on some distant horizon for you. 'Tis the only explanation for the things Mark and I have seen and why you spend so much time together. Though I do hope John Harris will do what is proper and speak to Mark about it. And that you both will consider yourselves and your need for wisdom and guidance."

Beth froze in her stance. How could it be that others knew of some untold future, yet she had no peace for a marital covenant, even if she did enjoy being with him? "There is nothing like that between us," she denied.

Judith laughed. "Come now. 'Tis not difficult to see when two people are falling in love. I'm one who knows. Mark and I courted after our fathers agreed, but we loved each other even before they gave their approval. We believed long ago we were meant to be together in God's holy name."

If only I knew, Beth thought. "But we are not the same people. Although Mr. Harris may believe what you say, I do not."

"Why?"

Beth had no answer. She hurried away, hoping to collect her thoughts and keep her own tide of emotions at bay before she felt herself swept away by it all. *Why don't I feel as everyone else does? Oh Lord, show me what I lack.*

❧

The large bonfire the Indians kindled warmed the chilly evening. Beth sat close to it with Rising Star by her side, wearing the new shell necklace the girl had made. This night, Wise One entertained them all with stories of the past, even of the large ships that once brought people like herself, Judith, Mark, and John to their villages. He talked of Manteo, who had befriended the white men and who eventually went to the white man's land across the Great Waters. Beth noticed the smile painted on Mark's face as if he were enjoying every bit of the story. Though they didn't know if the blood of the past lingered in this tribe or elsewhere, they had a peace that some of the colony had indeed found refuge. And for that, there was joy that their journey had not been in vain.

She glanced around to find John in the background, whittling at a stick with a sharp knife. Curly bits of wood fell under the knife's blade. He seemed preoccupied, as he had since the day they arrived. No doubt he was still anxious to leave the village. He had never been content while they stayed among the Indians. If only she knew what caused it. Why he could not be that friendly soul she had witnessed at various times on the trip but instead must turn into a man of disdain when confronting those he disliked.

She saw him move off, a silent and dark shadow with just the faint glow of orange from the firelight reflecting his sturdy form. After a time Beth stood, wished everyone a good night, and began making her way toward one of the lodges she and Judith shared with several Indian women.

The sound of her name uttered from the darkness stopped her. She saw John emerge from the shadows. He tossed away the stick he had been whittling and came toward her. She remembered the words Judith had spoken—how plain it was to see that they had forged a bond. But had they really? Or was it all still some dream?

"I haven't spoken of this. . . ," he began. "I'm not sure how to tell you, actually."

She stood still and silent, uncertain what he was about to say.

"I enjoyed very much the time we have spent together."

She sensed the warmth enter her.

"It means a great deal to me to know you care," he went on.

"Of course I do. We all do. We have to stay together when we make a journey like this. And you are our guide, after all. How will we return to Jamestown without you?"

John looked upward into the evening sky, just as the canopy of darkness began to fill with stars, and a sliver of moon materialized to give a bit of light. She watched him, sensing that his pain ran deep, deeper than the skies that held those stars. From whence came such sorrow, no one knew but God alone. If only he would speak aloud his thoughts while she stood waiting and hoping for them to be revealed.

"I've been thinking. . . ," he began.

Oh, can it be? Is he finally going to tell me what I have yearned to know about him? I knew some trouble lay hidden and unspoken. Dear Lord, may this be the time.

"We all have our quests on this journey. Your brother-in-law and sister have theirs. No doubt you have yours. And yes, I have mine. Would you like to know what it is?"

"Yes, I would," she said quickly. "I've been waiting so long for you to tell me. I know it's been hard these last few days, that you have held yourself back. But we needn't wait any longer. Let yourself go free in God's grace and tell me everything. 'Tis the right thing to do."

John's gaze immediately leveled with hers. He took a step back. "I—I didn't think you would want me to confess this to you. . . ."

"How could you think that? Of course I do. I just didn't know how to draw it out. Maybe I was timid. I don't want you to think ill of me."

He began to laugh. "Why would I ever think that? This is like a dream that has finally come to a place where it can be embraced and without fear." He stepped forward, his arms extended as if ready to draw her in.

Beth shook her head, retreating from his invitation. "John, I don't understand."

"Of course you do. I know now that our hearts are truly one, that we both think and breathe the same thoughts about each other. So now I can ask you, dearest Beth, to become my wife."

Beth gasped. Her hand flew to her mouth. "J–John." She could barely utter his name, so shocked was she at his proposal.

"I already know the answer, praise be, just by what was spoken tonight. Forever and amen, you are mine." He again stepped forward, his arms reaching for her, attempting to pull her into his embrace.

"I have hinted at no such thing!" She stepped away, turning from his confused gaze. "You didn't hear what I said at all."

"I heard every word—how you've been waiting for this time as much as I. That I needn't hold myself back any longer. It was like the feel of the ocean breeze to hear you say these words."

"Please. . .I. . ." She paused. "I—I can't marry you."

His arms fell limp. "What?"

"I can't marry you. Not after what's passed between us, or rather, what has not passed between us."

"Then what was all that just a few moments ago? About releasing ourselves to each other? Allowing God's grace to overcome? You even said you were waiting for me to ask."

"I wait for you to tell me who you really are, John Harris.

What burdens your soul? Oh, I've seen glimpses of your true self, yes. But I don't know you. The true man lies hidden behind some wall."

He whirled in a start, tossing his hands. "Beth, we have been over this so many times. Why must I confess everything of my soul before you will accept me? Is that to be the price for your hand?"

"Isn't truthfulness a worthy aim?"

He shook his head. "There are some things that I will not bare. . .not to you, not to anyone. You can't force my hand like this."

"Then I would say we both were mistaken in our judgment." She turned and made haste for the wooden lodging, refusing to look back.

Once inside, her hand touched her neck and the jewelry lovingly given to her by Rising Star. She felt no comfort in it. Despite what had happened between them, John filled a void in her heart. Without him, she was half-empty. But how could she have a marriage of dark secrets, where one couldn't trust the other? She took up the wool cloak he had brought from Roanoke Island. She pressed it close to her face, allowing her tears to dampen the garment. "Dearest Lord, what shall I do? Help me."

eleven

Depression was quick to settle over him. How everything could rapidly fade into some deep, dark chasm of no return, John had no idea. His mind was a whirlwind after the confrontation with Beth. Her words left a thorn embedded in his heart. For so long he had nurtured a desire to be with her and, ultimately, make her his forever. Now that he was spurned by her, the pain was even worse than the grief he held for the past. Once more, he faced another loss. Another good-bye. He couldn't understand it nor could he accept it.

The more he pondered the evening's conversation, the more confused he became. Why must he confess everything in his life so that she would find him acceptable enough to marry? Didn't he provide for her every step of the way during this journey? Didn't he see to her safety, her comfort, even hailing the good graces of womanhood God had bestowed upon her? Why then did she seek to dangle the wounds of his past above his heart?

She doesn't know you, John Harris, he reasoned. *She even said so. Who you really are.* He paused to consider this. *Who am I? A weary guide? A sojourner looking for his homeland? A wandering soul in search of fulfillment? A man entangled in a web of the past and unable to break free?* He thought of his good friend, Samuel, who often spoke of reconciling the past. Setting things in order. Finding the peace that eluded him. Now other things commanded his soul. He was a dark grave, as Beth once said. Only those looking from the outside in could see it.

Still he refused to reconcile it, to believe that Beth should accept his past. He had tolerated being in the Indian village for her sake alone. Now that she had refused to marry him, he saw no reason to remain in this place. He had done everything required of him as the role of a guide. He would leave forthwith and never look back.

John remained awake all night, even as the village slumbered. He watched the stars slowly drift in the night sky and the crescent moon rise and fall. To think of sleeping when everything in his life had no direction seemed absurd. He thought of Beth asleep with the other women. Maybe she felt at ease to sleep now that his claim to her had been dissolved. Or she rested knowing God held her life in His capable hands. But he could find no rest. He called upon God to help him in this hour, to make straight his path, to show him where he needed to go.

When the first birds began to sing and the village stirred to life at the rising dawn, John felt weary in mind and body. He watched through bleary eyes to see Beth emerge from the lodge, stretching her arms above her head as if to embrace the skies above. It pained him to see her loveliness after a night spent wrestling with his feelings. She moved toward a large earthen jar to splash water on her face. Only when she straightened, shaking free her hands, did her gaze lock with his. He thought she would turn away, but she did not. She simply looked at him, as he did her.

To his surprise, she moved toward him. "Good morning, Mr. Harris. How do you fare?"

"A bit weary, madam," he admitted, looking at his hands resting limp on his legs. "I could not find rest last night."

"I must say, neither did I."

His gaze again met hers, and she peered at him intently. How he wanted to nurture a hope that all was not lost, despite their conversation last evening. But he didn't want to succumb to the memory again. He refused to allow his heart the burden of bearing it.

"I think this is for the best," she continued. "I know we did not depart in the best of spirits last evening. But it will serve us both in the end."

"The only end I hope to see is what I asked," he said. The comment he uttered surprised even himself. Determination must be making its last stand.

"I'm sorry," she said gently, "but my answer has to be no."

Just then, Rising Star came to bid her good morning and accompany her to the cooking area where several of the Indian women were already making up cornmeal cakes for the morning's fare. She heaved a sigh and turned away from him, never looking back.

His eyes began to burn. He sighed with lasting despair. *This is the end, John. The time has come to make peace with the decision and embrace whatever lies ahead.* But without Beth to fill his life, the future looked bleak.

Later that morning, while everyone was engaged in the day's work, John looked about for his satchel of belongings. He had nothing of value, he knew, but a few possessions he might need as well as his trusty pistol. He took some of the morning's corncakes for sustenance and filled a leather pouch with fresh water from the water pot. He wondered if Beth could see his actions, but she had disappeared, likely with Rising Star to see the cornfields. They had already offered their farewells anyway. It was indeed the end of all things, and he would accept it.

"Are you going somewhere, Master Harris?"

He heard a voice behind him and turned to see Mark Reynolds looking at him and his bulging bag.

"I know the village is preparing to go on an expedition," Mark continued. "I thought I might try my hand once more at spearfishing." He chuckled. "It may be of great use for me to practice."

"I'm leaving," John announced.

"Good. I'll see you at the boats then?"

He shook his head. "You will not see me again, my lord. And since I have guided you here safely, I ask for the payment promised me."

The smile on Mark's face disintegrated into a picture of confusion. "You mean to say you are leaving us? Why?"

"I have my reasons, my lord."

Suddenly, Mark motioned him to follow. John resisted the gesture at first. He didn't want the man talking him out of his decision. But he also needed the money promised him, especially now that he was starting anew. He followed until they came to the lodging, where Mark disappeared. He soon returned with a small leather bag.

"You are an excellent guide, Master Harris," Mark said, handing him the purse of money. "I wish you well on your journey. Where will you go? Back to Jamestown?"

He shook his head. "No. I'm not certain where the Almighty will lead me, but it will be in the direction I need to go." He tucked the purse inside his leather belt around his waist. "Thank you for your sentiment." He could see the way Mark perused him, as if seeking out the manner of his soul. How he wanted to thrust up a shield to keep everything from the man's observing eye.

"I do hope you will find someone to whom you may

express what ails you, Master Harris. God gives us those with whom to confess and to pray. To uphold and to guide. To help make right whatever is wrong. He doesn't want man to be alone, as one of the islands we have seen, alone in some vast ocean of trouble. He gives us men to help in times of need. To hold us up as they did the arms of Moses when one is too weak to go on, and we are alone, contending with our adversities."

John said nothing.

"All of us have trials and temptations, you know. We can sympathize with them."

John gritted his teeth. "You have not had my trouble."

"No, I haven't. I'm the least to offer my feeble hand of assistance in times of need. But God is stronger. When one is sinking into the ocean depths and death draws nigh, sometimes the hand of God is the only source of rescue to be had. I read of explorers that drowned long ago while seeking this new land. One of them, Sir Humphrey Gilbert, was caught in a storm off Newfoundland that destroyed his vessel. And it was told that he said, 'I am nearer to God by sea than by land.' Even in death, he called out to the one Supreme Being to receive him. To know that his Lord was there, even in a sea of trouble when death came calling."

"I, too, called out to God when death came calling. I pleaded my case before His throne." John ventured to a fallen log and sat down with a thud. "He stayed silent to my confusion. To my question of why? Why did this happen?" Suddenly it tumbled out in a fury. "Why did my brother, Robert, have to die like he did? He was young and eager. Only sixteen. A bright young lad. Full of life for a new land. Full of adventure and a yearning to see and learn." The emotion welled up within. John could see that fateful day played out as if it were happening right before his eyes. He told Mark how he had gone off to follow what he thought was a deer in the wood back in Jamestown. And then he heard the terrifying scream. He raced back to find Indians scattering, some holding glistening tomahawks. And Robert was there on the ground, crying out for mercy when there was none to be had.

He shuddered, unable to bridle the tears that stung his eyes. "I came to him. He was trembling so badly. His blood was everywhere. He said, 'John, I'm afraid. I'm so afraid to die. Please, don't let me die.' I tried to talk to him, to help him, but his life slipped away. And he was gone. He was alive, breathing, whispering to me. And just like that, he was no more."

Mark said nothing, though John heard a swift sigh escape. He lifted his gaze to meet the man's before him. "So please don't fill me with tales of fortitude when death is at the door. My brother saw none of it with his dying breath. He saw only fear."

Mark paused. He then asked softly, "And what do you see, John Harris?"

John turned away to see several Indians in the distance among the lodgings of Sandbanks. He clenched his fist and gritted his teeth. He fingers felt for the pistol at his side. He knew what it was that rose up inside of him. Hatred. Rage. Vengeance. The need to spill blood. A life for a life. It flowed so strongly in him that he could barely hold himself back. If not for Mark's presence, he might have acted upon the temptation that wrestled with his soul.

"John, I could say much, but they would only be words in your ears. I can't offer any comfort for your heart. Only God can, and He must reveal His strength to you. But I do urge you to leave now, before it's too late. Find a haven. Allow God to heal you wherever you find rest."

John was surprised at the words Mark spoke. He thought for certain the man would try to keep him here. He would fill his mind with scripture he already knew—of allowing God to take vengeance, of casting his burdens upon Him—verses that would fall empty on a cold spirit like his. Maybe that's why John didn't want Beth to know. She would try to heal him, too, when he couldn't be healed. No mortal man could heal him.

He stood to his feet and shook the hand Mark offered. "Thank you."

"God be with you, John Harris. And look to Him who holds all of us in the palm of His hand."

❧

Try as she might, Beth could no longer stay apart from John without some manner of reconciliation between them. As time passed, her feelings for him only strengthened. He had been her protector, as he promised he would. He had shared about the land he loved. He had been there for her through everything. Was it fair that she kept him at bay because of some manner of trial in his life? That she could not show him mercy as the Lord would have her do? If only she could take back the words she had spoken. If she could have bridled her tongue and not pressed him as she did, driving him further away rather than closer to her. Often she thought of his proposal—how eager he was to have her in his life. And while she did once doubt her love for him, she knew now that she loved him and wanted him to be her husband.

She searched high and low for John that afternoon, hoping to steal him away and confess these thoughts that had been her constant companion. But strangely, he seemed absent from Sandbanks. Perhaps he had gone on another one of his expeditions, maybe even to Roanoke Island once again, though she felt certain she would have heard of such a trip.

At last she found Mark. He appeared melancholy and not his usual jovial self, staring outward as if deep in thought. For a time she thought he might be ill. "Dearest brother-in-law?" she asked gently so as not to startle him.

He stood at once to his feet. "Beth, I didn't hear you."

"What is it? Are you ill? Is it Judith?"

"No, I'm fine. But I fear one of us is gravely ill."

Beth clasped her neck in distress. "Oh, no! Is Judith sick? Oh please, may it not be the fever or the pox."

"No, she is fine. 'Tis not a plague of the body I fear, Beth, but an illness of the mind within John Harris."

Beth lowered her hand. "I don't understand. He is ill?" All at once she envisioned her father and his distresses of the mind.

" 'Tis not like what afflicted your father," Mark said as if he could understand her worry, "but something I fear will destroy Master Harris in the end unless the Almighty intervenes."

"Oh, no. I asked him if he could share his trouble. But he gave no sign at all. No eagerness. No will."

"Beth, John's younger brother was brutally murdered by Indians near Jamestown."

The statement he uttered was like a blow to her heart. She sank under the weight of it, not caring that her dress drowned in a sea of dirt below. She had known something happened between John and the Indians but never realized it could be something this tragic. "H–how did it happen?"

"He told me he had gone off to hunt a deer and heard the scream. When he returned he found his brother, the life draining from him, a cry of fear in his words. And 'tis that fear John cannot reconcile. That there was no peace in the death, but rather fear unlike any he had ever seen."

"This is so dreadful, I can't even say." Now she could clearly see why John refused to tell her. So terrible a circumstance would be hard to even utter, yet alone reconcile without the strength of God. "Oh, I want to comfort him in his time of need, Mark. Where might I find him?"

"He's gone."

"Gone!" She flew to her feet, gathering her dress about her. "No, he can't be gone! He can't!"

"There is nothing you can do but allow God to minister to his heart and give him peace."

"You mean leave him alone with such grief? Let him go mad? Or even die? No! You don't understand. I have seen how the afflictions of the mind can tear one apart. It can kill swifter than any sword. I can't let that happen to John."

Mark quickly grabbed her arm. "Beth, you don't know where he has fled. For all you know, he is on his way back to Jamestown. 'Tis better this way. He can make peace with himself and with God."

"He can't make peace. He's had all this time to make peace, even before we set foot in this land. And did he? No. We are the only ones who can help him." She lowered her head. "Perhaps we tried too hard. I fear it sent him away instead of drawing him near."

"All you can do now is pray. You can't find him here in this vast land. No one knows where he went. You must entrust him to the One who holds us all in the palm of His hand."

Beth shuffled off, her heart overwhelmed by sadness,

the tears flowing free. *If only.* She heaved a sigh. Maybe if she had said yes to his proposal that night, he would have shared the heavy burden of his soul. Maybe it would have been different. Now he was gone, and there was nothing she could do about it. She entered a forest of trees and a place of solitude. Mustering the strength, the words soon poured out. "Help him, God. Oh, help him, God. Please spare his life! Don't let this grief consume him. And help him know, somehow, that I care more deeply than even I knew. That I do want to become his wife. Oh, God, help him know my heart, wherever he is."

twelve

John didn't want to leave, but he had no choice. No strength. No will to remain, even if he did pause numerous times during his journey to gaze back down the sandy coastline to the village of Sandbanks where Beth remained. If he had the fortitude, he would sneak back that night and whisk her away from the place and the people who had bewitched her. He would take her to their own haven where they could bask in their love and forget about the past. But it was not to be. Her feet were firmly planted in the village, and his were directed by his circumstances. Neither would change.

He chose, then, to be a wanderer of both body and soul. A wanderer through the desert as Jesus had been. What he would find, he didn't know. Would the devil try to conquer him there as he had tried to do with the Lord and Savior? John prayed not. He murmured a prayer, even as the wind whipped sand into his eyes and snarled his hair. He coughed a bit, thinking of the scripture, how Jesus stole away into the desert for forty days with no means of sustenance. Maybe this was what he needed to do to be cleansed. To wander about without victuals or a place to go, wander until he could go no farther, when exhaustion would finally overtake him, and he would fall to the ground in complete surrender.

But try as he might, he could not get Beth out of his mind. He wanted to go back and tell her everything, that evil had taken away his flesh and blood. How he heard the cries of Robert in some nightmarish delirium and felt helpless to stop what happened to him. He knew Beth would reach out to him with compassion. Her arms would cradle him, her voice crooning as one might to a child, seeking to drive away the torment. But he could not revisit it all again, especially not with Beth. And because of this decision, she had refused him. There was only one thing left to do. Travel as far as he could away from the pain and seek out a new place and a new life.

Soon he came upon a place similar to where he and Beth had looked for the talking shells and marveled at the screeching gulls that flew in the skies. The birds were there to greet him, laughing all the while before settling down in the sand as if asking for his companionship. He could confide in a gull of his woes.

He sat down to watch the ocean roar and foam before him. Waves lapped the shore, coming closer and closer with each pass. The gulls toddled on their twin legs that appeared like fragile limbs, looking around, seeking a victual to share. "I have no food," he told the birds. "All that I had, I left behind, except for a few things in this satchel."

He opened it then and took out some papers. On one parchment, angry words spoke of a debt he owed back in England. The purse of money from Mark would cover that. The second note was from his father. Why he kept it, he wasn't certain. Nor was he certain why he took it out now to read.

My son, I beg you to reconsider what you are doing. The land of Virginia holds nothing. Your place is here, in our family fishing business, to continue what we have labored so long to bring forth. And yet, you wish to leave without my blessing. But in the least, you will not take Robert with you.

*He is to remain here, under my guardianship. In that, there
is no question.*

John's hand tightened around the paper. He had disobeyed
Father's order and taken Robert anyway. His parents would
never forgive him if they knew what happened. "No, they
would not," he said as a lone gull continued to keep him
company while the others flew off, calling to each other. "I
can't imagine a worse fate than telling them what happened
to Robert. Even though he was excited and begged me to
take him, it was my decision to have him disobey Father and
allow him to come with me." Perhaps the guilt was twofold.
Maybe he was seeing more than he had realized. Not only
the guilt for Robert's death, but also the guilt for having
brought him here against his parents' wishes. Could God be
trying to heal him, as Mark had said? Or simply allowing
him to wallow in further guilt and confusion?

John stood to his feet, crumpled up his father's letter,
and tossed it into the ocean. It played on the waves for a
moment until the water consumed it. "In this I rid myself of
the past," he said. "My father's directives. My love for Beth.
I toss it all away."

Suddenly the gull took flight, screeching as if in a warning.
John spun about to see several men, outfitted in heavy
armor, approaching. Instinctively, he felt for his pistol. He
soon recognized them as the same party he had met back on
Roanoke Island when he'd fetched the family's possessions.

"Ah, the one who rescued a fine lady's attire before we
could make sport of it," the first man said with a chuckle.
"Remember me? Anderson is my name."

"Yes, of course," John said, shaking the man's hand. "John
Harris."

"And I'm Edgar." The second man grunted, forcing a thick metal helmet from his head. "A grand sight indeed, this ocean. And not a soul to be seen anywhere about. We have been exploring these parts for several days."

"There are no white men," John agreed, "but there is an Indian village down the coast."

"Indians!" Anderson bellowed. "I thought they had long since left this place."

"They are still living there in a village they call Sandbanks. About a half day's journey south of this location."

"Are they friend or foe?"

"Friend, from what I've seen. Several even seem to have white men's blood in them."

The two explorers looked at each other. "From where, pray tell?" Edgar inquired.

"It is only an observation, but the family I led here believe the white men's blood may come from the lost colony of Roanoke."

The men burst into laughter. "Rather, you mean they have the colony's blood on their hands," Anderson growled. He brought out a snaphaunce pistol similar to John's.

"They are not a violent sort. They welcomed us. But I could not stay there any longer." John bent his head to see a few crabs skittering along the sand.

"Why?"

John glanced up to find the two men staring at him, ever curious. For some reason, he had no trouble confiding in them his hatred of the Indians at Jamestown for what they had done to Robert and how he would have nothing further to do with them. "But the family I led here insisted on staying at the Indian village. And since I have done what was required of me, I left."

"Too bad about your brother, my friend. I hear you, I do. The Indians are but heathen murderers, that's what they are. They don't understand that this land has been given to the white men by Almighty God, and we are the masters." Anderson stomped his foot to emphasize the point.

"Enough of this. Come show us this land, Mr. Harris," Edgar urged. "Do you know it well?"

"I know it," John said, even as they began walking along the shore. He took them north rather than south toward Sandbanks, glad for the friendly banter that temporarily rid his mind of the past. They talked of exploration, of the high cost in making such journeys, of the rumors of copper and other fine metals to be found in the area called Carolana, all for the gathering. But when they talked of the Indians, John said little. He would rather avoid the subject, even as they pressed him for more information about the Jamestown Indians and what they had done. When, at their insistence, John finally told them the details, anger filled the men.

"I killed an Indian once myself," Anderson boasted. "His friends came looking for me. That's why I came here. They can't be trusted."

For some reason, John thought of the Indians of Sandbanks; the girl named Rising Star; Wise One with his brownish hair and eyes so similar to those of a white man; the ones who talked of the white men as though they were friends. While he wanted to bask in the animosity shared among his fellow explorers, he considered the good things, things above, things they had done and his Beth among them. Rising Star and Wise One were innocent. And he had to admit, the other Indians of Sandbanks were innocent, too. They had nothing to do with what occurred at Jamestown. Then why did he possess some great boulder of anger, ready to thrust it at them and crush them to pieces? He swallowed hard. As if he had not already allowed that boulder to fall, even upon the one he loved. And the truth be known, he'd been crushed along with her.

"You have deep thoughts there, friend," Edger commented. "But tell us, is this a place where we can live?"

"I would like to settle here," John agreed. "But I don't want to settle alone."

"Nary a woman to be found in these parts," Anderson chided, "lest you fetch her from Jamestown fresh off the ships."

John nearly told them of Beth's existence, but stopped himself. Be they explorers, he knew, too, they were men as well, and he didn't want them stumbling upon her. She was his. Or she used to be his. He paused then, even as the two men continued on their journey, oblivious to the fact that he no longer walked with them. What was he doing? How could he leave her? How could he abandon the woman God gave to him by allowing grief to control his life?

"Are you with us?" the men called out.

John looked at the men. He turned and stared southward to where Sandbanks existed. No, he couldn't leave, not with everything he believed and the emotions he still carried. He loved Beth. He felt certain she loved him, too, despite what had happened between them. The separation would go no further. He would return, and somehow, by the grace of God, he would make her his wife. He would see that patience became his overriding virtue. And if he needed to confide in her concerning his past, so be it.

John shook his head. "I have duties to attend."

They laughed and asked what duties could beset him in this place of sand and sun. But John said no more. He would venture back to the village and along the way, think about what he would say when he saw her. He couldn't plead sickness of the mind or some numbing fear. He would say that love had returned instead. It could not be forced into submission, but rather it drove him to his knees. Love was able to conquer all, even the darkest and most depressing moments of life.

"Find us when you have come to your senses," Edgar said with a chuckle. "We will be going back to Roanoke Island and our party. Perhaps we will meet again as we explore more of this place."

John wished them well before turning southward, to the beckoning sounds of love on the wind and the roar of the ocean waves. He walked slowly, considering what was to come. Never in his life had he been put in such a place. If only he knew what to do when he arrived and how to confess the past.

Just then he heard Robert's pleading voice in his mind. It filled him, drowning the thoughts of Beth with the age-old grief once more. *John, I'm afraid. I'm so afraid to die. Please, don't let me die!* The ocean filled his mind, followed by a scream. It was the gulls again, but it could have been the Indians, screaming sounds of victory. He wavered and closed his eyes.

"Robert, I'm so sorry," he said aloud. "I'm sorry I took you here when Father told me not to. I'm sorry I wasn't there to help you when you needed me most. Forgive me." He sucked in the air. A bird suddenly landed at his feet. It wasn't a gull this time, either, but a different one. A dove.

His heart leaped. A dove of peace. Surely this was a sign from Almighty God. He sighed and closed his eyes, allowing the pain of the past to melt away. There must be more to all this than what he could see with his eyes. Things eternal. The peace that Robert felt at this moment, even if he felt fear before he left the world. Surely he was at peace in a place with no pain, home with his Savior. How then could he, John, be troubled in spirit?

John continued south toward Sandbanks, to the woman he should have never abandoned to this unpredictable place. His pace increased in his eagerness to see her again.

Suddenly he stopped short. Someone was approaching quickly, running toward him. He thought he saw what looked like a spear. He glanced wildly about and took cover behind some scrubby brush. He withdrew his pistol, checked the weapon, and waited. The figure stopped, breathing hard, glancing to the left and to the right. John could plainly see it was an Indian, with his sparse clothing and beadwork native to the Sandbanks village. In fact, the man himself looked vaguely familiar.

The Indian began to call out. John wondered what he was saying. He saw no one else besides the Indian. Surely it could not be an ambush. The man looked as if he had come alone. Slowly John came out from behind the brush.

The Indian paused. His eyes were large, the wind catching his long hair. He pointed wildly in the direction of Sandbanks and began speaking some frantic gibberish.

"I don't know what you're saying," John muttered, "But I don't intend to go anywhere with you." Then, to his surprise, the Indian came forward, waving his hand. Ignoring the pistol John held, he grabbed hold of John's arm. "What are you doing, you scoundrel! Let go of me." Even when he brandished the pistol, the Indian refused to waver.

Then he heard familiar words uttered from the Indian's lips. "Cold Man! Cold Man sick! Come. Come."

John froze. Cold man. Where had he heard that before? Colman! The Indians called Beth—Beth Cold Man. "Beth? Are you speaking of Beth? Where? Tell me where she is!"

"Yes, yes. Come." The Indian raced off, urging John to follow with words in his native tongue.

He had no idea what had happened and wished with all his might he could understand the Indian's mumblings. Even so, the words rushed out, short and raspy from the quick pace. "Is—is she hurt? Wh–where is she? What has happened?" The Indian said nothing more. John could not settle the rapid beat of his heart, both from the travel and the fear, which again reared its head to confront him. He tried to calm himself, thinking of the dove of peace at the water's edge. God desired peace to rule his heart and mind. To allow whatever happened to rest in His hands. But even as he considered these things, fear again wrestled with him, trying to prove the more powerful force. He fought to subdue it with everything in his being. John wiped the dampness that collected on his brow and drifted down his temples. He prayed like he'd never prayed before.

When they came upon the canoe the Indian had left, he entered and took up an oar along with the natural. He knew the canoe would bring them back swifter than walking. The Indian never stopped to draw a breath or drink from the leather water sack at his side. John found it difficult to keep up but did what he could, even as his throat became parched and his arms began to seize.

Finally, when they came to the bank, he expected to find Beth somewhere nearby. Instead, to his astonishment, the Indian left the boat and sat down on the ground.

"You can't sit!" John shouted. "To your feet, man! Show me Cold Man!"

The Indian only sat still and closed his eyes. Frantic, John searched the landscape, shielding his eyes from the intensity of the afternoon sun. How could the man stop here of all places? If what he said was true and Beth was in trouble, they had precious little time to waste. Pacing back and forth, John again shouted at the man. The Indian would not be moved. He only sat upon the ground as if in prayer. None of this made sense. But he refused to see some Indian cause another's death. He drew his pistol. "Take me to Cold Man now," he demanded.

The Indian ignored him.

John gritted his teeth. "Why do you do this? Don't you know a life hangs in the balance? Another life that I refuse to sacrifice to your confounded ways?"

Without a word, the Indian suddenly leaped to his feet and pointed. John whirled, dropping his gun when he saw several people in the distance. He moaned and raced over to find Mark there, along with several Indians. They stood hunched over a figure lying on the ground.

"Mark!"

The man looked up. His eyes were glazed, his face clearly broken by distress. "John."

"What happened?"

"It's a snakebite, John. Beth suffered a snakebite."

John looked down to find Beth with her face beginning to redden. He could see the poison already battling with her body. Then he saw deep gashes on her frail leg, the blood trickling down her pale skin. He whirled, watching an Indian clean the sharp blade of a knife. "What did that heathen do to her?" His hand brushed his side, and he realized his pistol was missing. He lunged forward with his fists clenched.

Mark held him back. "John, they helped her."

"They did no such thing. They. . .they cut her. . . ." *God, please, not again. I can't bear this. Not another life sacrificed to this place.* He struggled with his own pain even as Mark gently explained how the Indian had cut her leg to suck out the poison. His sight grew bleary, watching the Indians bind up her wounded leg. He fought to calm himself. The Indians did not seek death in this place. This was not Jamestown. This was Carolana where the Indians struggled to preserve the life of his beloved.

"Life and death in Creator God's hands," a voice pronounced. John looked over to find that Wise One had arrived from the village. "This yours," Wise One said, handing him the pistol. "My councilor find it."

John took it slowly. "So it was your councilor who came to find me at the beach. But ask him why he stopped when we were so close. He just sat down and would not move. I could have hurt him had I not seen you all here with Beth."

"You no understand. He pray to Creator God," Wise One said solemnly. "You need strength, man of fire, more than you know. You white men think you know everything. But Creator God know everything. You understand this, you do well."

John could not believe what he was hearing. He gazed at the pistol he held. He would just as soon cast it aside in light of the words Wise One had spoken, words that offered healing and hope. Instead he placed the pistol deep inside a bag of belongings, out of sight and away from his hand. God had sent His messenger in the form of this Indian to help when Beth and he needed it most. He now worked with the Indians to construct a litter to bear her up to the village. *Lord, I have made my peace with the past. Now please, I beg Thee, Almighty God, help my love get well.*

thirteen

She heard the voices all around and wondered where they came from. Perhaps they were angelic voices welcoming her into a heavenly realm. That was, until she felt intense pain. She cried out. *What is happening to me?* Voices of concern filled the air. Then came the touch of hands, first on her hand and then on her leg. She felt herself being moved, and suddenly the skies above moved as well. She was being taken somewhere, where she didn't know.

Oh, how she wanted to sleep. She was so tired. She didn't need to rest from fatigue, but something else, some weakness that gripped her body with tentacles that wouldn't let go. When she tried to speak, the words refused to come. Instead her face felt very hot. Her eyes burned. Her leg burned even worse. All she could do was pray. *Dearest Lord, I don't know what's wrong with me. I don't know what happened. Please help me. Oh God, what about John? Does John know? How I want him to know.* She felt the tears in her eyes. It was no use. John was gone. Gone like the flowers that fade after a brief time of blooming. Gone like her parents who were no more. Despite her effort, as weak as it was, she had driven him away when he needed her and she needed him. *Dear God, forgive me.*

❧

God, forgive me, John pleaded. How could he have let this happen? Again, he had turned away, and again, another one he loved was stricken. He tried to listen, even as Mark insisted this wasn't his fault. Beth wanted to go find him. It was her decision. But, he reasoned, she never would have left the safety of the village had he not walked away and left her. Despite Mark's words of comfort, this *was* his fault. He had not allowed Beth's concern to soften his heart. Now it was too late.

He glanced down at her still form, borne up by the litter they had constructed from a blanket and several stout poles. The Indians, led by Wise One, insisted on carrying the litter, even when he asked if he could help. Instead, he walked alongside Beth, praying for her all the while. When they paused to rest, he thought he saw a tear trickle down her face. He wanted to cry with her but held it back. She looked dreadful with her red face and damp brow. Like a brave warrior, she was fighting the poison within her. No pistol could fight such a battle. Only her will could do it.

"She is strong," Mark observed as John watched her face. "I don't believe this is her time to leave us."

"If anything happens to her, I refuse to live," John said quietly.

"Don't confess such things. We can do all things through our Savior Christ who strengthens us."

"But I can't do this. Not again. I will not lose another."

"John, you must realize this was her decision. If you could have seen her determination to find you, to risk whatever danger lay ahead. She blamed herself, as you now blame yourself. She believed she had driven you away. That mercy failed to reach you when you needed it. I daresay you both are more similar than either of you ever considered."

Mark chuckled then, a strange sound to be heard at this somber time. But the words ministered to John's confused and hurting heart. In them, he did find a reason to rejoice, that he had not been wrong when he sensed he and Beth were meant for each other, that his quest, his journey to love, had not been in vain. God, in His wisdom, had brought them together, and now He must restore her so their journey might be completed.

When they arrived at Sandbanks, it appeared the entire village came out to greet them. Immediately Beth was whisked away into one of the lodgings. A leather flap closed, sealing Beth from view, even as an old Indian woman wagged her finger and spoke harshly to him. John knew what she meant—that he was to remain outside while they tended to Beth. He maintained a vigil by the lodging, waiting for any news. Rising Star came by with another beaded necklace she had made, but even she was turned away by the old woman.

Now the young Indian girl came and sat down beside John. He didn't know what to say to her. But looking at her large black eyes that stared up at him, he could sense her worry. "She will soon be well," he told her.

"I pray," the young girl said. "I pray to Jesus."

John stared at her. "You know about Jesus? Who told you?"

"Beth Cold Man. Say He Great Spirit of love. Say He heal like Great Spirit."

"Yes," John said, recalling the scripture that teaches that by His stripes one finds healing. He confessed it aloud, even as Rising Star sat patiently beside him. He found a soothing presence in the young girl, who seemed to help him in his faith, especially when tested in these murky waters of anxiety.

When John saw the leather flap rise and Judith emerge from the tent, he immediately stood to his feet. "What do *you* want?" she asked, her gaze leveled at him, her face rigid as stone.

"Is there any news of Beth? I've heard nothing."

"Yes, there is news. For all we know, she could die. How could you do this to her?"

John stared. "Madam, I—I don't understand."

"This all happened because of you! Beth went after you because you left the village. Oh, why did you make her fall in love with you? You don't understand how sensitive she is. How she always wanted someone to love her. . .and now she could die because of it. If only you had left her alone and not wounded her heart." Judith bent her head, allowing her tears to flow unabated.

His throat closed over in a hard knot. He found the words difficult. "I—I'm sorry for all of this. Truly I am. I—I didn't know she would come after me. If I had known, I never would have. . ." He paused. "It doesn't matter. None of this can be changed now. The only thing that matters is that she gets well."

"If she dies, I will have no one left at all. No one, don't you understand? I will be alone." She hurried off, the sound of her weeping echoing in his ears.

John looked back at the lodging where Beth lay inside, battling for her life. How he wished it were he in there instead of her. He would gladly have taken the snakebite and more.

Finally, after another agonizing hour passed, he could stand it no more. He simply had to see her. He lifted the animal skin that covered the doorway. Inside it was dark. He could barely make out the figure lying still on a bed made of poles and skins. When the old woman noticed him, she tried to shoo him away.

"No. I will see Beth Cold Man."

Reluctantly the woman stepped aside and allowed him to

enter. A strange poultice lay on Beth's stricken leg, which had swelled to twice its normal size. Her breathing was labored, her face red, her dry lips moving. He stared long and hard, maintaining his silence, though inwardly he groaned. *God, if only I had known. If only she had given me a glimpse of her true heart. I never would have left. I would have stayed forever and waited as long as need be.* He heaved a sigh, watching the old woman come and change the poultice. "What is that?" he asked, pointing to the strange bandage.

She muttered in some foreign tongue. Then suddenly he heard the answer spoken in English.

"Red elm."

John turned to see that Wise One had also entered the lodging to stand by his side.

"Will. . .will she live?" he asked.

He shook his head. "No one know. No one but Creator God."

He looked back at Beth's feeble form, once so vibrant and alive, now teetering on the precipice of life or death. "She must live."

"Not for us to say. Only Creator God know."

"I thought you would believe in many gods," John muttered. "All this talk of Creator God. Who told you about God?"

"A white man long ago. He came with book and taught many things. It has been passed down. Many in village believe in Creator God. He true God. One God."

"Three persons in the Father, the Son, and the Holy Spirit, but One God," John added.

Wise One nodded. "And see? She hears your voice."

John looked to find Beth stirring. He slowly approached. "Beth?"

She then appeared to drift off once more into a land of peace, away from the pain and misery of life.

"Patience," Wise One said.

Patience. How he needed that along with faith. He sighed and retreated from the lodge to find the daylight slowly melting away with the coming shadows of evening. If only a new dawn would arise. If only the night would stay away and instead, the sunrise would come. But night would fall and, as Wise One said, he must patiently wait for a new day.

❧

Bright sunlight assaulted her eyes from the open doorway. She was in her room of stone at Briarwood, waiting for Father to call for her and Josephine to come with the morning bread. She stirred and tried to raise herself. She felt the pain in her leg and opened her eyes. Above her, a face peered into her own. It was wrinkled and dark, with large dark eyes and a swath of black hair fastened behind at the nape of the neck. This woman wasn't Josephine but some strange woman who even now fumbled with something on Beth's leg. Beth wanted to scream but forced the reaction away.

Suddenly everything came back to her in a tumult. The conversation with John when he asked her to become his wife. The utter sadness when she learned he had left after she told him no. Her voice begging Mark to go with her as she went seeking John by the great ocean. Then the pain of something on her leg and her screams at seeing a snake with its fangs tightly embedded in her flesh. *I was bitten by a snake,* she told herself. *Oh dear God, help me! Will I die?*

She tried to raise her head, but it felt like a large stone. She looked around for a familiar face, especially for the one she had sought to find when the snake found her instead. *John, oh, John. Where are you?* Tears slid down her cheeks. *Even now, when I'm so ill, you won't come. Oh, why?* She closed her eyes, hoping to bury away the pain of the bite and the agony in her heart. She was too late. Too late for love. Too late for life. Too late for everything, it seemed. She wanted to have a good, long cry, but even that proved too tiring. Everything took effort, even trying to reason out what had happened to her. *If only John were here. If only he could know that I care. . . that I love him.*

Then, just like that, he was there. Tall, commanding, dressed in the billowing shirt she found so appealing. She wanted to weep for the sight of him. Was it really him or some feverish delirium? It must be the fever. He couldn't have known about the snakebite. He had left, perhaps to meet up with the other explorers, journeying far away from her and from the love they could have enjoyed together. She turned her face to the bark walls comprising the lodge, unwilling to witness such a vision that tore her heart into pieces.

Then she heard his deep but gentle voice. "Beth."

She forced her head to turn. It was so slow to obey. There stood her vision once more. And then it spoke again to her.

"I'm here," the deep voice said gently.

John? You can't be real. Oh, dear God, please don't punish me with the sight of him. It's too much to bear. But his large hand that rested on hers felt alive with the warmth of life's blood flowing through it.

"Beth, I'm here," he said once more. "It's me, John. I will never leave you again. I will be here to protect you. Always."

John, oh, John. It is you!

❧

When he came in to see her the following morning, she was sitting up on the bed of skins, her eyes bright and alert, and to his astonishment, a smile lighting her face. "You look much better."

"I feel better, thanks to Rising Star's grandmother who knows medicine." She scrutinized the poultice on her leg. "Though I must say this poultice smells terrible."

He looked at her for a time until he found her returning his gaze. He immediately set his sights elsewhere. For some reason, he found the words difficult. What could he say after all they had been through? He knew he could no longer bring up the idea of a marriage covenant. But he still remembered that she had sought him out, even after her answer had been no and he had left. Surely that meant something was still alive within her, some manner of care, some bit of love left over to embrace.

He sat down by her bed. All at once it came to him, the words to say through a symbol of a covenant between God and man. He brought out the wooden cross he had whittled long ago in Jamestown. "I made something for you." He held it before her eyes.

"Oh, John, it's beautiful."

His lips twisted into a lopsided smile at her eagerness and the way she spoke his name.

She examined it carefully. "I know how much you like to work with wood. I've seen you whittling. God has given you a gift."

"My father always wanted me to be a fisherman, but I must say that I do like to work with wood. I considered one day that I might apprentice with a furniture maker or another of that sort." He chuckled. "But what is a furniture maker to do in a place like this?"

"I thought you only liked to explore."

"I do, but I like to create, as well."

She smiled. "I can see how the two are linked. God's work is a heavenly creation in the way of the ocean, the talking shell, and the seabirds."

"He made them all for us to enjoy."

She held up the cross. "And so, too, you like to make things for others to enjoy. I think you should become a furniture maker, John. There must be someone in Jamestown who can teach you the art. When we return, perhaps. . ."

He shook his head. "I can't go back to Jamestown, Beth."

She set down the cross, her eyes widening at this news. "Please don't say you are leaving again!"

"No. I won't leave, as I promised. Whether I'm to remain in this area or even Roanoke Island, I'm not certain. But I know I must stay here."

"Even if I ask you to go?"

Her question cut him to the quick. "Beth. . . ," he began. He felt the draw upon his heart, even more so as the deep color of her eyes pleaded with him. "I've betrayed my heart to you, and so I will not speak of it again. I will look to God who holds my life in His hands, wherever that may be."

Beth laid the cross beside her on the bed of skins. "Thank you for the gift," she said softly. "I must rest now."

He stood to his feet, bidding her a gentle farewell before stepping out into the brightness of a new day. Yet he couldn't help thinking of her words that echoed in his thoughts. *Even if I ask you to go?* He considered, again, the idea of an apprenticeship in the skill of furniture making. But the lure of this land, the ocean, the sands, all beckoned strongly to him. It had never faded, even with the time he spent in Jamestown. He loved this land of Carolana. He admitted he loved it as much as he loved Beth. If only he could have both.

fourteen

Beth was thankful for the quick return of her strength. Now able to move about the village, she smiled at the Indians who came to greet her. Rising Star became her constant companion, often fetching what she needed and then remaining by her side. Through their encounters, Beth talked more to the young girl about the Savior and found a captive audience to anything she wished to share. But the time she spent with John brought her the most happiness. He seemed a different person, as if he had made peace with his past. Though she often wanted to talk about that time, she restrained herself. She felt certain John would speak of it when he desired.

"We go see shell that speaks?" Rising Star asked one day while sitting by Beth's side as she worked on weaving a basket. Since stricken by the viper's bite, Beth had taken to learning other crafts to pass the time. The thick rushes that grew by the ocean made perfect tender from which to construct baskets. Though at times her hands became raw from the strips, she enjoyed the work.

"Not today," Beth said. "I know I'm better, but I think I still need more time."

Rising Star gazed longingly at the small trail they used to make their way toward the great ocean. Beth smiled at her eagerness. "My shell no more," Rising Star mourned. "Give it to another. Want more."

"You should have kept it. But I promise, as soon as I'm

better, we will ask Mr. Harris to come with us and look for other shells. He knows the perfect ones." She sighed, for the mere thought of such a journey made her insides tingle. Yes, he did know the perfect shells. The perfect scenery, by the ocean waves. And yes, the perfect way to kiss by the roar of the ocean, even if she had been blind to it all. She picked up another reed, ready to thread it through, when she heard the rumble of thunder—or rather, the steady hum of some deep voice greeting her.

"You seem better, madam."

She glanced up, blinking at the full sunshine in her face. She saw the outline of a tall figure standing above her and the ever-present shirt that reminded her of clouds drifting in the sky. "Quite. And I am a bit handier these days, as well." She picked up a basket for his inspection.

"Perfect." John stood unmoving and silent. His presence filled her with warmth.

"And what are you doing this day? Staying out of mischief, I hope?"

"Indeed. I daresay your brother-in-law will try to convince me to do some spearfishing."

"Good! I expect you will return with a bounty for our dinner."

Again he only stood as a tower, the sun outlining his solid form. "Beth. . . ," he began.

She looked over at Rising Star beside her. "Rising Star, go see if there are more reeds. I only have a few left to work with." She held up the reeds she needed.

The girl nodded and pranced away. John chuckled, settling himself down beside her. "You can read my thoughts."

She laughed. "I could never do that, Mr. Harris. You're a man who buries thoughts deeper than anyone I have ever known—with the exception, perhaps, of my own father."

"I'm trying not to keep those thoughts hidden but to reveal them to those who care." He picked up a slim reed and ran his finger across it. "I haven't spoken of the past, but your brother-in-law told me you knew."

"Yes. I'm dreadfully sorry to hear about your brother. You can't possibly know my grief for you."

"I think I do know. Anyone who would come after me, taking such risks, and then suffering a snakebite for me knows well. And she has a merciful heart beyond what one could hope or think."

"I prayed for that," Beth said softly. "I prayed God would give me a merciful heart, that I would understand and not condemn. I wanted to be a part of your life, John. Not just in the corner of it, lingering there, but right in the middle. Only it seemed you didn't want me there to share in your sorrow."

"I know, and I was wrong. I didn't really know the treasure sitting right before my very eyes, of one who cared enough to share my pain. You've had pain in your life, as well. You can sympathize with sorrow. I don't know why I was blind to it."

"We're not without our own enemies of the soul," Beth said. "Even scripture speaks of the pain of this life. But we can lay it all to rest, knowing God is the great victor." She watched as he rested his hand on hers. She did not stir, even as he leaned over to greet her with a kiss. This kiss proved more wondrous than the first, sealing a future covenant between them. There was no mistaking it, no driving it away, but only an eagerness on her part to embrace it.

All at once, they were jarred apart by some commotion stirring within the camp. Several Indians raced by, shouting at each other, pointing to the trail that led toward the beach.

"Something's happening," John murmured in concern, helping Beth to her feet.

Just then, Beth saw Wise One stride forward, his face a picture of concern, his fists clenched.

"Wise One, what has happened?"

"White men come to the village," he said. "They have taken one of our own!"

Beth and John exchanged incredulous looks. "Stay here, Beth," John told her. "I don't wish you in danger, and you're still weak." He soon disappeared among the Indians, whose voices rose in fear and uncertainty. Beth began to pace, unable to believe what was happening. She prayed the first prayer to come to her lips. "Oh merciful God, help us!"

❧

John didn't know what to make of Wise One's announcement but entered the lodging where he kept his bag of meager belongings. He retrieved his pistol and tucked it into the belt around his waist. He joined the throng making haste down the trail until he stopped where they had gathered. Before them stood several white men, two of whom he recognized. They were Anderson and Edgar. To his horror, Rising Star stood between them, trembling. Sunlight was reflected in the tears on her face.

"Surely one of you heathens here speaks English!" Anderson shouted to them all. "Meet our demands, and she goes free."

"What is it?" Wise One said.

"Ah, I knew it! See?" Anderson said, slapping his cohort on the shoulder. "One of them does know English. Well, you see, we like your land here. A fine place indeed for a new village, a white man's village. So we're commanding you to leave your village."

"No! We no leave. This our land."

Anderson chuckled. "You don't understand, do you, Chief? If you don't leave, then we're obliged to keep the heathen girl for ourselves. We could use a good cook in our camp."

"This our land," he repeated. "We no leave." He paused. "Offer much. Beads. Fish. Corn."

"Not interested."

Wise One raised his hands. "No leave land of our fathers."

"Then I guess you don't care if you ever see this young thing again." He shook Rising Star's arm. She seemed to faint in his presence. "Let's be off, then."

John pushed through the crowd of Indians. "Anderson, wait!" he shouted.

Anderson stepped back in surprise at the sight of him. "Well, if it isn't John Harris."

Edgar hooted in agreement. "Glad to see that you came here ahead of us. You never told us what a fine place this is. Plenty of good land and a village to establish our presence here, with the water to our back and the ocean before us. Everything we could want."

"Let the young girl go. You don't need her to get what you want."

Edgar and Anderson looked at each other in surprise. "What's this?" Anderson retorted. "Surely you of all people aren't defending the likes of these murdering heathen."

"They've done nothing to you. They are innocent. Let her go."

"Innocent? The Indians have done plenty to you, or did you forget already? Murdered your own flesh and blood, they did! How you watched him die before your eyes. And now you can stand there and defend the likes of them? Stand with us instead."

A tremor seized John. He wavered. If only they had not brought up the pain once more. *Robert.*

Just then he felt a brush of wind. Out of the corner of his eye he saw Beth venture forward to stand by his side. "Beth, no," he whispered fiercely. "Please go back."

"No. We stand together, John. You and I. I won't have them deceive you like this." She linked her arm through his.

He gently removed her arm. "Please, I don't wish you hurt. Please go back."

She stepped back but a few paces, remaining just behind him, in his shadow, rigid in faith, with the strength he desperately needed at this moment. "Don't let them do this to you, John," she said. "Remember. Please!"

"So, Harris, what say you?" Anderson shouted. "Are you going to stand with us in the memory of your fallen brother? Will you defend his honor? And what better way than to declare this place for the white man, eh?"

John looked over at the Indian tribe that had gathered. Their dark eyes focused on him. He could see Rising Star's mother there, the grief written on her face, her eyes pleading with him. Then, the face of Wise One, standing firm, his arms crossed before him, his feet planted as if refusing to be moved. Just beyond him stood Mark and Judith, with Mark gently shaking his head no, his hand extended as if begging John to relent.

"Yes," John agreed, redirecting to Anderson and Edgar. "If you will allow me to come parley with you about the matter and you set Rising Star free in the meantime."

"Surely, though we keep the heathen girl with us as our bargain until they leave. We think it only fair."

John hesitated. "I will speak to the village councilors." He then noticed Beth's startled expression.

"John, what are you doing?" she cried. "You can't let Rising Star go with them! Have you lost all reason?"

"Please have faith, Beth. And say no more."

He nodded toward Wise One, asking him to summon the elders for a meeting. They gathered in a group, even as John kept the corner of his eye trained on Edgar and Anderson with Rising Star between them.

"Why you do this?" Wise One said sternly to John. "Now must we withdraw as the price of my councilor's daughter? We no do this. There be war first."

"I will not let anything happen to Rising Star, as God is my witness. But if we raise a confrontation now, many will be hurt. Maybe even killed by their fire sticks. They are not easy men with whom to parley. They mean to take what they wish. But there are other ways. I will go with them and seek an agreement to the matter."

"They are here for evil. And they have the daughter of my councilor."

"I swear upon my life and upon the Word of Almighty God that she will be safe. Let me deal with these men, for they are explorers like me. And if I fail, you may do as you wish."

Wise One nodded. John returned to address Edgar and Anderson. "Come, let us talk. The Indians are considering your proposal. And in the meantime we can eat hearty and discuss the matter."

"We are not changing our minds, Harris," Anderson warned. "And the Indian girl stays with us."

John said nothing, only murmured a prayer for guidance, even as he glanced back to see Beth's worried expression. He did not know what he would say or do when they arrived at the explorers' camp. He could only pray to God for an answer that would win back not only Rising Star but also keep the village of Sandbanks.

They didn't have to travel far before John came upon the base camp of the explorers. The other men of the party who had gathered around a fire immediately came to their feet upon their arrival. They inquired about the native girl and what Anderson and Edgar were up to.

"She's our bargain, she is," Anderson commented, accepting the cup offered to him. "If the heathen don't leave their village, she's ours."

Just then, John saw a man step forward, dressed in dark clothing. "What is this?" the man demanded. "Who is this poor child?"

"We are only keeping her for safety, Reverend," Edgar said. " 'Till the Indians leave, that is."

"And why must they leave? Have you informed Captain Browning of your deeds this day?"

John's ears pricked at this information. Captain Browning. So the men did have a leader among them. "I would like to speak to the captain, if I may," he said.

"And you are. . . ?" the reverend inquired.

"John Harris. Fellow explorer. A friend of the Indians."

Edgar and Anderson scoffed at his words. "He don't need to be telling our business to the captain," they both said at once.

"Anything having to do with this mission is important," the reverend said. "Please, Master Harris, come this way."

John found himself scrutinized by every eye as he made his way past six other men to the rear of the encampment and a shelter erected in the distance. There he met the lanky Captain Browning with a large map spread out before him.

"Captain, may I present Master Harris," said the reverend.

"To what do I owe the pleasure of this meeting, Master Harris?"

" 'Tis a grave matter I seek, sir, having to do with two members of your party—Anderson and Edgar. They have taken a young Indian girl captive, demanding an exchange for Indian land. They claim to do your bidding. So I have come to negotiate a compromise, if you will."

Browning put down his quill. "You must be mistaken, Master Harris. I gave specific orders that the naturals be offered compensation for their land. We favor its location in the marshland, you see."

"Captain, if I may say, there are plenty of equally fine areas to establish yourselves. The Indians only inhabit a small part of the Hatorask region. Surely you can find another place just as suitable."

"Not from what my men have reported to me. How is it you know the land so well?"

"I have been here many times, Captain. In fact, I led a party here myself from Jamestown a fortnight ago. If you wish, I will help you find a better place."

"Captain, the Lord would have us do well among the naturals of the land," the reverend added. "Are we not here to keep the peace and not brandish the sword? Can we not do better here than at Jamestown?"

"I have no intention of bringing forth a conflict, Reverend Robins," the captain said. "We were only to bargain with the Indians."

"A conflict you will have, sir, if your men do not release the Indian girl whom they are using as part of that bargain," John said. "She is the daughter of one of the councilors, and the Indians mean to make war if necessary to gain her release."

The captain frowned. "I did not give orders for captives to be taken." He called to the sentry. "Have the Indian girl released at once to Master Harris's guardianship. And bring me the offenders that I may deal with them."

Edgar and Anderson were hurriedly brought to the captain's tent. "Sir, we thought you would agree to our plan," Edgar began when Browning confronted them. "You trusted the matter to us."

" 'Tis a plan wrought by fools," he snarled. "We are not here to take land by force. Others have done so and were massacred, as it was in Jamestown and beyond. Now it may yet bring an Indian war party upon us for your foolish act."

"There is no need to be concerned," John assured the captain. "The head councilor of the village, Wise One, only wishes to live in peace with the white men. His village even cared for stranded men long ago. We think perhaps they might have once given shelter to survivors of the lost colony."

"And you dared to incite a rebellion with these people?" the captain bellowed to the two cowering explorers. "You will be dealt with in the utmost severity. Sentry, keep watch on them." He then turned to John. "I beg forgiveness for this matter. And I would like it indeed if you might show us other areas that would do well for settlements."

"If I may say so, sir, why not here? You have the sound to your back and the ocean before you. The land is good. 'Tis no different than at Sandbanks, I can assure you."

The captain looked about, even as John exchanged a small smile with the reverend.

"Aye, as it is with most things in life that lie right before our eyes. I will consider it. But if not, I do ask for your help in seeking another place."

"Certainly. And if you wish, sir, you would be most welcome to come parley with Wise One of Sandbanks, in whom you will find a beneficial ally in this place."

"Thank you, Master Harris. Without your help, I daresay we might have only brought blood upon this land instead of new beginnings. And our very names would have been cursed for all time." The captain offered his hand, which John shook.

Outside the shelter, the reverend likewise shook his hand. "Praise be for miracles!" the reverend exclaimed. "If I may ask, I should like to visit this village of Sandbanks. My desire has always been to reach the lost with God's saving message. And here you have made the way for me, Master Harris."

" 'Tis not my doing, Reverend, but the hand of a merciful God." John sighed then, thanking God for His blessings, even as he saw a joyful Rising Star run to embrace him.

*

Beth remained awake, refusing to allow sleep to claim her. She had heard only fragments of John's plan and wondered what would happen. She hugged her arms close to still her trembling, thinking of Rising Star and John among those hate-filled men. Ever since the confrontation, she prayed for them and for her own strength to bear up under it all. She prayed they would call on God to help, that somehow through this they would all grow in their faith. But at that moment, her faith rested in God and the man named John Harris, the one who once despised the Indians, the one who listened as the men taunted him about his fallen brother and then urged him to side with them. If only she had confidence in this night and in John's wisdom. Even if her confidence waned at times, she could trust in God and

His power working through John. God would not abandon them in their hour of need.

Rising Star's mother came to her then, a sad figure in the darkness, with the flames of the fire illuminating her distressed face. The Indian woman drew close to Beth as if seeking shelter from uncertainty. She began to mumble words in her native tongue. A bit of English came out of the woman's anxiety. "What they do?" she asked.

"I don't know," Beth told her, "but I do know John will do everything he can to bring Rising Star home safely. He cares for her as I do." She knew this to be true. He had said from the beginning he would protect and defend. And she believed he had experienced a change of heart, that anger no longer ruled him. She squelched her rising tide of doubt by placing her trust in him, for the first time in her life.

For a good part of the night, Beth and the Indian woman kept vigil by the fire kindled between them. Soon Judith and Mark came to join them, searching the darkness as Beth did, with only the call of insects and the sound of their anxious breathing to break the stillness. They sat side by side, shivering from the steady breeze, waiting for what seemed like hours, each of them thinking and praying. Only when they saw the flicker of torchlight and the sound of voices did they spring to their feet and head down the trail to meet the returning party. It was John with Rising Star and a stranger wearing black.

Rising Star's mother took the young girl in her arms, weeping for joy. Beth shook her head in wonder, staring at the wide grin painted on John's face.

"I'd like you to meet Reverend Robins," John said, stepping aside. Beth welcomed the stranger accompanying them—a short man dressed in dark clothing.

"A pleasure, madam," he said with a smile.

"Thanks be to God and to the reverend here," John said. "God was with us. And, thanks be to God, the captain of the exploration party was a man of sound mind and godly character. He made amends for the foolish actions of his men. Now I only need go with them on the morn to find another good place, and the matter is settled. Lest they find the land they now dwell in to their choosing."

"Praise be!" the reverend added.

Beth could only marvel over what had happened. Joy filled her heart, even as she followed John to the water pot. There he dumped water on his head from a large shell. "Ah, that is good."

"I can't believe this," she murmured, watching the water trickle through his hair and down his face. " 'Tis a miracle, John."

"I must say I'm amazed as well. I thought for certain I might have walked into a trap. Or onto a path of no return. But when I met the reverend upon arriving at the camp, I knew God was with me. And speaking of the captain, he is not unlike me, a man who wishes to settle in peace and without the bloodshed we have seen in Jamestown."

"Oh, John! So the men relented their claim to the land?"

"I told them there was plenty of good ground for them to build a separate village elsewhere, that the white men and the Indians could live peaceably together. That we could live as brothers—and the reverend agreed."

"John, I don't know what to say." Beth stared at him for the longest time, seeing the goodness flowing from him like milk and honey. How she loved him with all her heart. At one time she thought that Judith had found the perfect man with his merciful heart and the righteousness of God permeating his being. But now she knew she was blessed beyond measure to have John Harris for her own. She sighed. If only she did have him. The covenant still needed to be revived. How or when, she did not know.

❧

The next day was marked by thoughtfulness and contemplation. At high noon, the Indians put on a feast with much food and drink to celebrate the return of their beloved daughter, Rising Star. During it all, Beth saw John off by himself as he had done when they first arrived, whittling on a stick. Only this time he seemed content, with a smile on his face, as if he had found his own special place among it all.

Beth slowly approached him. When she did, he directed a smile toward her. "This is indeed a time to rejoice." He showed her another cross he had whittled. "I will give this to Rising Star as a token of remembrance." His smile faded away. "But it seems my lady has some other matter on her mind?"

"John, I'm sorry to say this. . . ," she began.

Immediately he stood upright as if ready to face yet another plague upon his being. "Beth? Is something wrong?"

"There is still a matter that must be dealt with," she said.

"What?"

"If you don't know by now, John Harris, then I think we still need a long talk between us."

He appeared confused. "I don't understand. Have we not spoken openly? I've kept nothing else in secret, if that is what you fear. I've tried to lay everything open to you."

"We have accomplished our quest in this journey. But now I wish to know of your own personal quest."

He chuckled, and his smile returned. "Ah. My own quest. Miss, you needn't concern yourself with it. I'm quite fulfilled. . . ."

Immediately she sensed sorrow at these words. She thought he would leap at the idea that she hinted at a marriage covenant. But had that all changed, too? Was it now lost forever?

". . .Or rather, I *will* be fulfilled if you were to remain by my side forever. And so I ask if—"

"Yes!" she interrupted with glee.

"But I haven't yet finished my question to you," he said, his voice expressionless but his eyes twinkling in merriment. The chuckle rising up within him played like music to Beth's ears.

"You have indeed, Mr. Harris, who is my personal guide in matters of the heart. And my answer to you is—yes, forevermore!"

fifteen

"Dearest Beth, you must hold still if you want me to put this on right," Judith said, rearranging the wreath of flowers in her hair.

Beth tried but couldn't help shuffling her feet in anticipation. She felt Judith's hands steady her, a broad smile filling her sister's face as she secured the wreath to Beth's head. For so long, Beth had dreamed of a day like today, when she would meet her love and accept his hand in marriage. And now it was about to happen, with the man she met here across a wide span of ocean, to the very place where he had been waiting. Even now, she could picture John waiting anxiously by the tribal fires, along with the reverend, who had been with the other explorers and who, since the incident with Rising Star, had taken up residence within the village of Sandbanks. She sighed, thinking how perfectly Almighty God had arranged everything. Only He could have done it. Only He could have known the secrets of the heart and brought her the perfect man to fulfill her deepest longing.

Beth whispered a prayer to calm herself. In the distance, she could see the villagers gathering to watch a white man's ceremonial marriage. No doubt they were curious. She was thankful Reverend Robins was here to conduct the ceremony. She could not help but giggle over it all.

"Why do you laugh, Beth?"

"Oh, Judith. . .to see how much God loves us all. And to think, even with the explorers who came seeking mischief, the Almighty used it to bring a man of God here to Sand-banks who can conduct our marriage."

" 'Tis indeed a wonder," Judith agreed, stepping back to observe her. "And you, dear sister, will be a wonder to your husband-to-be."

Beth felt for the ring of flowers cradling her head and touched the necklace of shells about her neck, a gift from Rising Star. When they heard the beat of a drum, Beth came forward slowly toward the array of people, both white and Indian, assembled before God to witness a covenant of love. But at that moment, Beth's gaze turned away from all the well-wishers to center on the one she loved with all her heart. Their eyes met. Their gazes lingered. A small smile fell across John's lips. His face glowed in the sunlight. He wore the billowing white shirt she loved. When his hand grasped hers, she felt peace and joy in the same instance. Facing the reverend as one, they spoke their vows and were married before the eyes of Almighty God and the witnesses there gathered.

After the proclamation was given, cheers arose from the masses, led by Mark and Judith. They grew into a tumult that echoed throughout Sandbanks. Drums began to beat. Indian children danced in circles. Women laughed. Beth felt the embrace and tears of her sister, who gave her a kiss.

"I'm so happy for you," Judith whispered.

"I am, too," Beth admitted, with a sideways glance toward her new husband. John received handshakes from Mark and good wishes from Wise One and his councilors, who rewarded him with a pipe, feathers, and an earthen pot filled with seed corn.

"May Creator God shine upon you," Wise One said solemnly.

John bowed before the Indian, who seemed to have aged in the weeks they had been there. "Thank you. May His face shine on you and this village as well." John then took up Beth's hand as if to share in this hope with her. She welcomed his touch, especially when she began to think of their new life and all the challenges yet to face.

At that moment, Rising Star came up to greet them. At first Beth smiled until she noticed the girl's cheeks glistening in the sunlight. They were wet with tears. "I miss you, Beth Cold Man," she said. "I ask you not leave, but I know you do."

"Yes. But we will see each other again someday. God keep you in His tender care."

Rising Star dried the tears from her face and held up a shell. "Talking shell," she said proudly. "The one we see at water. I get another. So I give to Beth Cold Man to remember."

Beth couldn't help but laugh as she took the shell, thinking how much it had shown love to her—first by a man who used it to display the wonders of the sea, to the time when she showed the love of the Creator God to Rising Star. "John, look. It's our shell."

He took it and held it up to his ear. "It's playing the same music we once heard and kissed to, my dear."

She giggled before thanking Rising Star for the gift. The girl nodded, shyly backing away until she ran off to her mother's lodging. There were more gifts, earthenware, even a pair of leggings for each of them, and fine beadwork. Looking upon it all, Beth couldn't help but feel sadness. Soon they would leave this place, she felt certain. Perhaps to return to Jamestown and establish a fine plantation on the James River. But she wondered of her promise to Rising Star. Would she ever see the young girl again?

❧

"You are very quiet," John observed. "Too much excitement for one day?"

Beth glanced over to see but a glimpse of John's face, the rest of him overshadowed by the night. He was propped up on one elbow, staring at her. How she did love him. It had been a sweet time together after the ceremony, with the Indians giving them their own lodging for the night. But once more she sensed a new part of her life waiting to be written. The next chapter that began with this marital covenant. As it happened once before in England upon the death of her father, she now wondered about the future. What should she do? Where would they call home?

" 'Twas a wonderful day," she said with a sigh, intertwining her fingers through his. "I only wonder about our future. Where we should go and make our home?"

"I'm quite certain I know," he said quietly.

She glanced over at him. Surely he couldn't know her thoughts, though she had heard from Judith how much she and Mark often came up with the same idea in the same instant. Not that she had any idea for the future. There were only four possibilities. Return to England from whence they came. Go back to Jamestown where they had first met. Find another place to dwell within Virginia or Carolana. Or stay here in the village. But none of them seemed right.

"You want to go back to England," he said solemnly.

She stared at him in surprise. "Why do you think I want to go back there?"

He shrugged, stroking the top of her hand with his thumb. "I remember how you were when we first met. Unsettled and unsure. You looked as if your heart remained in your homeland."

"Do you have people waiting for you there?"

He shrugged. "My parents. They would be sad for certain to know what happened to one of their sons."

"But what happened to Robert was not your fault."

He hesitated. "Yes, it was. My father told me not to take Robert. He went anyway."

"But did you steal Robert away out of disobedience to your father, John? Or did he come willingly?"

He twisted his lips. "Actually, Robert sneaked aboard the ship. But I didn't tell him to leave, either, when I found him. He begged me to take him."

"Then it was your brother's decision to go. And you did all you could for him. Cease blaming yourself for this. He is at rest."

John sighed. "And what about you? Are you at rest?"

Her head found a place of comfort on his shoulder. "If you mean at this moment, yes. And I have no desire to return to England. When I left Briarwood, I left it forever and took my heart with me."

His hand caressed her hair. "Then we can at least say that the New World is now our world. So where would you like me to build you a home?"

She opened her mouth to offer an opinion, only to quickly shut it. If only she could know his thoughts. Where he truly wanted to be. She thought long and hard. Then she saw it. His blue eyes sparkling at the mention of Hatorask. His gaze encompassing the vast ocean. His large hand scooping up the talking shell. His first kiss as the waves came forward to lap at their feet. It seemed so plain to her eye at that moment. "I think I know what to do," she began, "but we've only been married a day. I want this to be our decision, not one or the other."

"I agree. It needs to be from our hearts."

They remained quiet, each thinking and listening to a heart beating rapidly, accompanied by the sound of insects buzzing outside the dwelling.

Then it came at once like a chorus of hearts turned into one.

"Hatorask?" they both said.

Beth and John broke out into laugher before their arms found each other in a tender embrace.

"Hatorask it is," John said with glee.

Peace filled her heart. Yes. Hatorask, indeed.

❧

"We shall miss you dreadfully," Judith said with a sigh as they gathered together for their final meal. Beth could hardly swallow down the morning's cornbread for the thought of leaving her sister. Mark and Judith would be returning north to Jamestown, while she and John would be drifting toward Roanoke Island in search of a place to build a home. "There is no one here, Beth. No other women. And no church."

"The reverend has said he wishes to remain in this area," John added. "We are already seeing people coming from the north. This is a wide-open land. It won't be long before there are settlements."

Beth could see the longing on Judith's face. She didn't know what to say. "Jamestown is but a few weeks' travel," she added with hope. "John knows the way. We will see each other again."

Judith barely touched her breakfast. The distress on her face was evident. Beth then realized what plagued her sister. They were all that was left out of the family. All they had was each other, and now they would be separated.

"I think 'tis best we get ready," Mark told Judith, gently ushering her to her feet. "We have found another Indian who can guide us back to Jamestown," he said to John.

"And what of your quest, sir?" John inquired.

"There are still questions left unanswered, Master Harris. Answers known only to God, I daresay. But I'm very much satisfied with the conclusion, that is, the new Indian friends we have made and the new brother-in-law I welcome."

John smiled, even as they both shared a hearty handshake.

Judith embraced Beth. "I shall miss you dreadfully, dear sister. A few weeks' journey seems so far away. But I know God has you in His tender care."

"Good-bye, Judith." With a sigh, Beth stepped back. Judith returned to her possessions, hardly giving her another glance, as if it proved too painful. Slowly Beth made her way to where John had assembled their belongings, along with a few Indian porters who would help them bring their possessions to a canoe resting in the water.

"You don't regret your decision. . . ," he began in concern.

The distress must be evident on her face. She lowered her eyes and managed a smile. "Of course not. Judith is all the family I have left. But I know we can't be far apart with God watching over us both."

He nodded, though quietly observing the moroseness that plagued her. When they began the trip, Beth soon forgot about the emotional departure and concentrated instead on a new land. When they arrived at the place where they had first shared their kiss, she asked John to leave the canoe there. They approached the beach to find the waves rolling against the shore, bringing with them many shells that would whisper their welcome.

"This was an interesting journey here," she marveled. "And now we can claim this place for God and for the Harris name."

"The Harris name?" he wondered.

"Of course. A blessed name, and I am the most blessed woman."

He chuckled. "I'm glad you found joy in this journey. 'Twas difficult for me, I must say."

"But look what we found at the end. New discoveries. Friends. Healing in our times of greatest need. Love. More than anyone could ask or hope."

"Praise be to His name," he said softly, gathering her in his arms. "So are you ready to call this land of Hatorask ours?"

"Yes, dearest John. Let us begin."

A Letter To Our Readers

Dear Reader:
In order that we might better contribute to your reading enjoyment, we would appreciate your taking a few minutes to respond to the following questions. We welcome your comments and read each form and letter we receive. When completed, please return to the following:

Fiction Editor
Heartsong Presents
PO Box 719
Uhrichsville, Ohio 44683

1. Did you enjoy reading *Journey to Love* by Lauralee Bliss?
   ❑ Very much! I would like to see more books by this author!
   ❑ Moderately. I would have enjoyed it more if

   _____

   _____

   _____

2. Are you a member of **Heartsong Presents**? ❑ Yes ❑ No
   If no, where did you purchase this book? _____

   _____

3. How would you rate, on a scale from 1 (poor) to 5 (superior), the cover design? _____

4. On a scale from 1 (poor) to 10 (superior), please rate the following elements.

   _____ Heroine   _____ Plot
   _____ Hero   _____ Inspirational theme
   _____ Setting   _____ Secondary characters

5. These characters were special because? _____

_____

_____

6. How has this book inspired your life? _____

_____

_____

7. What settings would you like to see covered in future
   Heartsong Presents books? _____

_____

_____

8. What are some inspirational themes you would like to see
   treated in future books? _____

_____

_____

9. Would you be interested in reading other **Heartsong
   Presents** titles?   ❏ Yes   ❏ No

10. Please check your age range:
     ❏ Under 18   ❏ 18-24
     ❏ 25-34   ❏ 35-45
     ❏ 46-55   ❏ Over 55

Name _____

Occupation _____

Address _____

City, State, Zip_____

Virginia
WEDDINGS

3 stories in 1

*E*xperience life and love
in the beautiful Virginia
hills as three women live
through the challenges of
romance.

Historical, paperback, 352 pages, 5³⁄₁₆" x 8"

Please send me _____ copies of *Virginia Weddings*. I am enclosing $6.97 for each.
(Please add $3.00 to cover postage and handling per order. OH add 7% tax.
If outside the U.S. please call 740-922-7280 for shipping charges.)

Name_____

Address _____

City, State, Zip _____

To place a credit card order, call 1-740-922-7280.
Send to: Heartsong Presents Readers' Service, PO Box 721, Uhrichsville, OH 44683

Heartsong

Any 12
Heartsong
Presents titles
for only
$27.00*

HISTORICAL ROMANCE IS CHEAPER BY THE DOZEN!

Buy any assortment of twelve *Heartsong Presents* titles and save 25% off of the already discounted price of $2.97 each!

*plus $3.00 shipping and handling per order
and sales tax where applicable.
If outside the U.S. please call
740-922-7280 for shipping charges.

HEARTSONG PRESENTS TITLES AVAILABLE NOW:

(If ordering from this page, please remember to include it with the order form.)

Presents